GLADIATOR SCHOOL

BOOK 3

BLOOD & SAND

DAN
SCOTT

SCRIBO

A division of Book House

First published in Great Britain by Scribo MMXIV
Scribo, a division of Book House, an imprint of
The Salariya Book Company
25 Marlborough Place, Brighton, BN1 1UB
www.salariya.com

Text Copyright © Dan Scott MMXIV

ISBN 978-1-909645-16-5

Book Design by David Salariya

Special thanks to Rachel Moss

© The Salariya Book Company
MMXIV

Printed and bound in India

The text for this book is set in Cochin
The display type is P22 Durer Caps

www.scribobooks.com

GLADIATOR SCHOOL
BOOK 3

BLOOD & SAND

DAN SCOTT

SCRIBO
A division of Book House

ROME, AD 80

To the Campus Martius

Forum Romanum

Velabrum

Pons Aemilius

Tiber Island

Forum Boarium
& Portus Tiberinus

Trans Tiberim

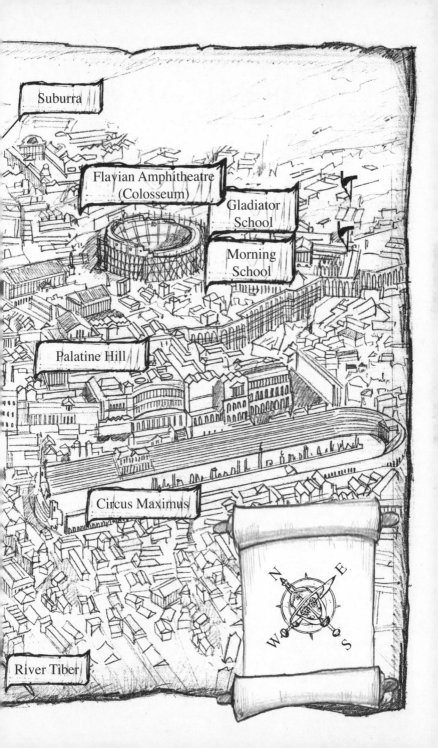

Introducing Gladiator School, a series of novels set in a rich and textured world of dusty arenas, heated battles, fierce loyalty and fiercer rivalry. Follow young Lucius as his privileged life is suddenly turned upside down, leading him to seek answers amongst the slaves and warriors who work and train at Rome's gladiator school.

Reader reviews of Gladiator School 2: *Blood & Fire*

'There are fights in dusty arenas, traitors, disappearances, family loyalty, criminals and gladiatorial games. All very exciting and a great adventurous read for kids that like a bit of action and a bit of history in their novels. My son said these books were really exciting.'
BECKY GODDARD-HILL, BOOK REVIEWS FOR MUMS

'Pompeii itself is accurately described . . . as a rough-and-tumble almost "frontier" town . . . Scott has also obviously carefully researched the stages of the Vesuvian eruption and expertly worked them into the plot line. Once more suspense propels the narrative and narrow escapes should keep young readers turning the pages eagerly.'
MARY HARRSCH, ROMAN TIMES

'The story continues with all the attention to compelling detail that won it so many fans. Action adventure, Romans, gladiators and so much more, brought to life for readers of 9+ in a series that captivates readers both young and old.'
GERRY MAYFIELD, OUR BOOK REVIEWS ONLINE

**What the lovereading4kids reader reviewers
said about Gladiator School 1: *Blood Oath***

'I would not put it down.'
GRACE PARKER, AGE 10

*'It's brilliant; it has a mix of different genres so it is
suitable for everyone. You will love it!!!'*
CHRISTOPHER TANNER, AGE 11

*'It made me feel like I was actually in Ancient Rome
with Lucius.'*
LUCY MINTON, AGE 9

*'There is only one single bad thing about this book
and that is that it ends!'*
ADAM GRAHAM, AGE 9

*'I . . . liked the way it told you what the Roman word
meant in English – it was really interesting.'*
CARLA MCGUIGAN, AGE 12

*'If you like adventures with a touch of mystery you
will love this book.'*
SAM HARPER, AGE 9

*'I was sitting on the edge of my seat wondering what was
going to happen next.'*
SHAKRIST MASUPHAN-BOODLE, AGE 10

THE MAIN CHARACTERS

Lucius, a Roman boy

Quintus, his older brother

Aquila, their father

Ravilla, their uncle

Caecilia, their mother

Valeria, their young sister

Isidora, Lucius's friend, an Egyptian slave

Agathon, a freedman, formerly pedagogue
(tutor) to Lucius and Quintus

Silus, beastmaster (supplier of wild animals to
the amphitheatre)

Crassus, a lanista (trainer of gladiators)

Eprius, a young nobleman from Pompeii

ROME
AD 80

THE STORY SO FAR…

Until the age of thirteen, Lucius Valerius Aquila had led a happy, comfortable life as the middle child of a well-to-do Roman family. His father, Quintus Valerius Aquila, was a respected senator, and they lived in a luxurious villa in Rome.

All that changed one day in early July, AD 79. That was the day Lucius's father disappeared, just in time to avoid being arrested for treason. Lucius would never forget the sight of the soldiers marching into their house, searching through their personal belongings. The soldiers claimed that Aquila was the Spectre – the ruthless informer whose reports on private conversations had sent many people to their deaths under the previous emperor, Vespasian. Now the new emperor, Titus, was determined to end the practice of informing. Lucius knew his father had always hated informers, and he was sure he was innocent. Yet everyone else, his family included, seemed to accept that Aquila must be the Spectre.

And with Aquila gone, along with all his money, Lucius and his family had to face the sudden loss of their home, wealth and status. Lucius's uncle, Gaius Valerius Ravilla, became their protector. He sold off their beautiful villa, their slaves and most of their possessions, and installed them in a cramped flat above a smelly fast-food shop in an unfashionable part of Rome called Suburra. In these new surroundings, Lucius's mother Caecilia soon became a gloomy shadow of her former self, and his little sister Valeria grew ever more frustrated and irritable. But his older brother, Quintus Valerius Felix (known to his family as Quin), caused the biggest shock when he announced his intention to support the family by becoming a gladiator. This meant renouncing his citizenship and taking on slave status – but Quin, who loved the guts and glory of the arena, relished the prospect. He persuaded their uncle Ravilla to give him a try-out at his gladiator school, the Ludus Romanus.

Quin adored his new life as part of the school's familia (troupe) of gladiators, and made rapid progress with his training. But Lucius, like Aquila, had always hated the games. He was desperately worried that Quin would be killed, so he got himself a job at the gladiator school, hoping to keep an eye on his brother when he wasn't cleaning the gladiators' rooms and running errands for the school's lanista (trainer), Crassus. The work was both strenuous and dull. His only consolation was his budding friendship with an Egyptian slave girl called Isidora, who also worked at the school.

Lucius missed his father intensely and longed for a return to their former life. One day, to his great surprise and joy, he received news of his father. Rufus, a new fighter at the school, revealed himself as Aquila's personal slave. He told Lucius that Aquila had been forced into hiding by the allegations made against him. Aquila knew where proof of his innocence could be found, and he needed Lucius to help him get hold of it, as he could not risk returning to Rome himself.

But before Rufus could lead Lucius to his father, Ravilla had him put to death. It turned out that Ravilla was not the kindly uncle Lucius had taken him for. Ravilla hated his brother Aquila and was glad that he'd been forced into exile. The last thing he wanted was for Lucius to prove Aquila's innocence.

With Rufus's death, Lucius was now sure that Ravilla was behind the accusations against his father. He was determined to expose his uncle's role in the affair and prove his father's innocence. He just wished he knew where his father was, so that he could make contact with him.

To help him in his quest, Lucius knew he could rely on the friendship and support of Isidora. In her previous job as a slave in Ravilla's household, Isidora had suffered more than her share of Ravilla's brutality – he had tortured and killed her parents. Since meeting Lucius, she had helped show him exactly what sort of a man his uncle was.

But before Lucius could continue with his search for the truth, there came an unwelcome announcement: the Ludus Romanus had been given the honour of representing Rome at a festival of games in the city of Pompeii, a whole week's march to the south – and Lucius and Quin would be among those going.

But Lucius was to learn much more in Pompeii than he had ever expected. On his first day there, he was recruited to work for the local worthy who was sponsoring the games – Marcus Nemonius Valens. At first Valens seemed very friendly, but Lucius soon discovered that, like Ravilla, he had another side to him. At the same time, he learned something truly shocking about Ravilla.

One evening, at a party at Valens's house, he overheard a private conversation between the two men, in which Valens accused Ravilla of being the Spectre. To Lucius's amazement, Ravilla admitted that he was. Lucius knew that his uncle was a corrupt and deceitful man, but it had never occurred to him that he might actually be the Spectre himself. This made his accusations against Aquila even more monstrous. He must have accused Aquila of being the Spectre both to destroy his brother and, at the same time, cover up his own guilt.

Valens was blackmailing Ravilla – threatening to expose his secret unless Ravilla paid him. Lucius soon found out that Valens knew everyone's secrets in Pompeii, and this was how he made his money.

Lucius told all this to Quin. But his brother refused to believe that Ravilla was the Spectre, believing instead that Valens was a villainous liar. He resolved to expose him before the crowds at the arena that afternoon. But Quin was overheard by one of Valens's spies, and, after winning his gladiatorial bout, he was stabbed by the man he had bested (another Valens spy) before he could say anything incriminating. Later, as Quin was being treated by the surgeon, one of Valens's thugs poisoned him.

Meanwhile, a young seer named Atia was warning that the gods were about to destroy Pompeii. Her warnings, combined with a series of terrifying earthquakes, were enough to convince Ravilla to order the gladiators' early departure from Pompeii. But before they could leave, Mount Vesuvius erupted and they were forced to take shelter in their barracks from the rain of volcanic stones. The bombardment caused a wall to collapse, and Quin, already wounded and sick from poison, was entombed under the stones. Miraculously, when they dug him out, Quin seemed to have recovered much of his health – perhaps the absorbent volcanic stones had somehow helped purge the poison from his system. Lucius, Quin, Ravilla and the rest of the gladiators' familia managed to escape from Pompeii just before the city was engulfed in a fiery surge from Vesuvius. Valens, however, perished along with all his dark secrets. Ravilla, so it appeared, was safe once more – and the proof that Lucius sought in order to clear his father's name seemed as far away as ever…

REBEL ELEPHANT

ROME
1 MARCH AD 80

ucius had spent the entire morning trying to coax an elephant to kneel before a statue of the emperor Titus. He was having no luck. He raised his ankus – a training stick as long as a man's arm – and slid it down the back of the great beast's foreleg, but the elephant remained stubbornly upright. She had knelt happily just a few minutes earlier and had received a bucketful of tasty roots for her pains. But, for some reason, when faced with the square-jawed features of the most powerful man in the known world, she always opted to stand.

Personally, Lucius found it hard to blame the creature for refusing to show the man respect. After all, it was his imperial agents who had stolen her from her homeland in Africa and brought her here to this strange and frightening city. The elephant, so Lucius had been told, had been driven into a pit by Numidian hunters, then fed only barley juice for days to subdue her. In her weakened state, she had been transported in a shuttered cage across land and sea to the port of Ostia, then taken on a barge up the River Tiber to Rome. How terrifying must the crowded, noisy docks have seemed to this gentle animal reared in the tranquil expanses of the African plains?

Since then she had spent her days here at the vivarium in the Trans Tiberim* district of the city, on the western bank of the Tiber. She had been trained to do tricks – to throw spears in the air, stand on upturned buckets, and fight bulls. And she'd had to get used to a much more crowded and noisy world than her old home. Her enclosure was a cage of closely spaced bars, just ten paces to a side. It was one of hundreds of similar cages in the vivarium, each of which contained beasts from across the empire. To the elephant, it must have seemed a loud, smelly and terribly alien place. Did she ever think about what she had lost – the forests, the muddy lakes, the wide open spaces, and the herd she had left behind?

Lucius checked himself. It was a fault in him to get sentimental about the animals in his care. He had even gone so far as to give some of them names.

* *vivarium: a place where live animals are kept and raised. Trans Tiberim: Across the Tiber; this area to the south of Rome is called Trastevere today.*

16

(He'd decided the elephant was called Magnentia.) He wished he could be more hard-hearted. After all, there were to be no happy endings for any of these beasts and he'd best get used to it. They had been brought here to Rome for one reason only: to perform, to fight and ultimately to die in the arena. In four days' time, the Inaugural Games of the Flavian Amphitheatre were due to begin. The night before, the animals of the Trans Tiberim vivarium, and all the other vivaria dotted around the outskirts of the city, would be loaded into reinforced wagons and transported to underground vaults beneath the amphitheatre to await their debut in the show.

Lucius was about to give Magnentia another gentle prod when the door to the enclosure suddenly burst open. Silus, Lucius's boss, strode in. The beastmaster was a large, thickset man with a gleaming bald head, a thick beard and dark, angry eyes. As always, he clutched a coiled length of rope in his right hand – a bullwhip – ready to flick at any animal he felt like hurting at that particular moment. Silus enjoyed hurting animals – or so it seemed to Lucius. He used his whip randomly and without reason. He was violent, unpredictable, and all the animals were scared of him. As he came in, Magnentia trumpeted fearfully and bolted towards the far corner of the cage. In so doing, she knocked over the statue of Titus. It fell with a clatter to the floor and broke into half a dozen pieces.

'Stupid creature!' bawled Silus. He unfurled his

whip and lashed her with it. The iron tip made a loud crack as it landed on her side. Magnentia bellowed with pain. He lashed her once again, and then a third time. Each time she roared her pain and tried to wedge herself further into the corner. Lucius cringed as he saw the dark red marks left on her skin.

Seemingly satisfied with the punishment he'd inflicted, Silus wiped the sweat from his brow, gathered up the whip and stuck it in his belt. 'The dumb brute has no idea how much it cost to get hold of that statue – nor what a crime she's just committed in breaking it.' He turned to Lucius. 'You, my lad, are going to have to repair it, even if it takes you the rest of the day. Understood? Have you got her to kneel before it yet?'

'Er... no, sir.'

Silus's nostrils flared impatiently. 'What in Jove's* name is wrong with the animal? Those Numidians swore she was the most intelligent of the herd. And it's true, she hurls weapons like no elephant we've ever had. I've seen her kill two bulls with a single thrust of her ivories. So why won't she kneel?'

'She *does* kneel, sir,' said Lucius. 'Before you managed to find that statue, I was getting monkeys to crouch in front of her, and she'd kneel before them every time.'

'So she's prepared to submit to a monkey, but not to our emperor, is that what you're saying?' growled Silus. His hand moved to his whip – his automatic

* *Jove: another name for Jupiter, the father of the gods.*

response to anything that annoyed him. 'Maybe she needs to learn the price of such disrespect…'

'No, sir,' pleaded Lucius. 'I think she's learned that lesson already today. Just give me a bit more time. I'm sure I can get her to do this.'

'We don't have much more time, boy,' snarled Silus. 'In four days' time, the emperor will appear on his podium at the opening ceremony of the games, and this elephant must kneel before him. This is my gift to him, and if she doesn't do as I demand, I will personally disembowel her with a blunt knife and turn her tusks into toothpicks. Understood?'

Before he left, Silus turned back to Lucius. 'Oh, and by the way – no food for her for the next twelve hours.' He pointed at the broken statue. 'That man is a living god, and I want her to feel the consequences of her blasphemy.'

PART ONE

THE LETTER

CHAPTER I

1 MARCH

When he was alone again with Magnentia, Lucius went over to her and gently stroked her enormous ear, something that always seemed to comfort her. She made a snuffling sound and leaned in against him. Close up, her tusks were huge and yellow, and sharp as spears. He'd seen her gore bulls with them, but he wasn't scared – she was always gentle when she wasn't fighting for her life.

He went to the stable and fetched a large bucket of water. From a shelf stocked with herbs and medicines, he found what he needed. While Magnentia sucked noisily from the wooden bucket with her trunk, Lucius tenderly dabbed at her wounds with a cloth soaked in terebinth resin, then smeared them with soothing aloe vera cream.

'What are we going to do with you, my girl?' he murmured. 'How are we going to get you to do this one simple task?'

Lucius remembered the words of an old elephant trainer from the East (a 'mahout', as they call them over there), who had been working at the vivarium when Lucius first arrived. 'A good elephant keeper', he said, 'has to slip into the elephant's skin. He has to feel and behave as an elephant does.'

Lucius was wondering how it might be possible to slip into an elephant's skin when the door to the enclosure opened again. This time it was his friend and co-worker, Isidora. She was small, tough and wiry, having lived all her thirteen years as a slave. She and Lucius had worked together at the gladiator school until last winter, when Ravilla, who also part-owned the vivarium, decided, quite suddenly, to move them there.

Isidora took one look at the broken statue and the scars on Magnentia, and sighed. 'Silus has paid you a visit, then?'

Lucius nodded.

'And Magnentia still won't kneel before the emperor?'

'No, for some reason she won't.'

Isidora started to giggle, then stopped when she noticed Lucius's frown. 'I'm sorry, but I find it hard to take all this very seriously. You Romans like to make gods of men and expect animals to worship them. In Egypt we know that it's the animals who are the gods. Your emperor should kneel before Magnentia!'

'You must find this whole set-up pretty grotesque in that case?' said Lucius.

'You mean rearing animals for slaughter for the entertainment of the masses? Yes, I do.' Isidora's velvety brown eyes flashed with anger. 'But it's the Roman way, isn't it? You're never content simply to rule. You constantly have to prove your power – over people, over nature. And thousands of innocent animals will have to die for the sake of your arrogance.'

Lucius was used to Isidora's anti-Roman rants. Perhaps she was right, but he wasn't going to give her the pleasure of hearing him say it. Besides, the Romans had done some good as well, hadn't they? He hadn't heard Egyptians complain too much about the roads, the baths and the temples the Romans had built for them, nor the security the Roman legions provided for their merchants and traders.

Crouching down in the dust, Lucius picked up Titus's arm and tried to fit it back onto his shoulder. 'I'm going to have to find some glue from somewhere,' he muttered, getting up.

'I'll come with you,' said Isidora. 'Farewell, Magnentia, you big, brave beauty.' She waved at the elephant, and the two of them left the enclosure and began walking down one of the long aisles that separated the various animal pens and cages in the vivarium. From behind the barred walls came all manner of sounds: snuffles, snorts, growls, barks, hisses, howls, roars and almost human screams.

Lucius had been working at the vivarium for several weeks now, but had not yet got used to the constant cacophony, nor the sheer range of wildlife that had been collected here from the furthest reaches of the empire. It seemed that almost every day a new shipment of exotic beasts arrived on the barges that came up the Tiber, and Lucius could only marvel at the imagination of the gods in devising all these strange and varied forms. He'd met a few of them before, such as the crocodile, lion and giraffe he'd seen at Valens's menagerie in Pompeii. But he had not been prepared for the sight of animals with humps on their backs (Isidora told him they were camels), monkeys with the heads of dogs (baboons, she called them), spotted dogs called hyenas that laughed as if you'd just cracked a rude joke, snakes as long as Silus's bullwhip and as thick as a gladiator's thigh, and rhinos – enormous armour-plated beasts with horns on their noses.

Isidora seemed to take it all in her stride, yet not a day went by when she wasn't complaining about something or other. If she wasn't grumbling about Rome 'stealing' the crocodiles, hippos, camels and baboons from Egypt, she was blaming the 'cruel and incompetent' trappers and traders for the weakened state of the poor animals when they arrived.

'Sometimes I wish we were back at the gladiator school,' she remarked to Lucius as they walked along the aisle. 'I find it easier to watch people hurting each other than hurting animals.'

'The gladiators have no more freedom than the animals,' Lucius pointed out.

'No, but at least they understand the situation they're in. These dumb beasts will go to their deaths in a state of fear and bewilderment... Ravilla knows how horrible it is here at the vivarium. I think he sent us here as a warning.'

'What sort of warning?' asked Lucius, surprised. His uncle had been remarkably friendly lately. Perhaps this wasn't surprising, as everything appeared to be going his way. Valens, the only man with the power to destroy him, had perished during the eruption at Pompeii. Aquila, Ravilla's hated brother, languished helplessly in exile. Meanwhile, the emperor had handed Ravilla a senior role in the organisation of the Inaugural Games. Ravilla's star was definitely on the rise, which would account for the thin-lipped smile Lucius found fixed to his uncle's face whenever he saw him these days.

'He wants to demonstrate that he has complete power over us,' said Isidora. 'He knows you overheard his conversation with Valens – that you know he's the Spectre – and he assumes you've told me about it. By sending us here, he's saying: "Look, I can change your life in an instant. And if you ever even think of crossing me, your fate will be no better than one of these animals."'

Lucius had told Isidora everything that had happened in Pompeii. It was typical of her to take the bleakest view.

'How can Ravilla know that I heard him?' he asked.

'He overheard Quin mumbling about it during his fever, didn't he? Or Crassus could have told him.'

Appius Seius Crassus was the lanista at the Ludus Romanus, so he was quite close to Ravilla. Lucius had forgotten that he'd told Crassus about the conversation – and, of course, it was possible that Crassus had passed this on to Ravilla during one of their private meetings. Still, he wasn't convinced that Isidora's theory was correct. It was far more likely that Ravilla had sent them to the vivarium for the simple reason that they were needed there. The animals were arriving thick and fast, and the staff needed all the help they could get with feeding and caring for them.

A low growl to their right made Isidora pause. The most dangerous animals were housed in a double-walled enclosure – a cage placed within a timber surround. 'How's Kato these days?' Lucius asked warily.

'I don't know,' Isidora replied, her voice now thick with anxiety. 'He's better than he was, but still poorly.'

Kato was an injured tiger that Isidora was trying to nurse back to health. The trappers who'd caught him in the forests bordering the Caspian Sea had injured his left forepaw, which had then become infected during the journey to Rome. Silus, typically, had wanted to destroy him – he couldn't see the point in feeding and caring for what was clearly a dying animal. But Isidora had persuaded him to wait a further week to see if the tiger recovered. The week was due to end tomorrow.

'It took me three days just to get him to trust me, so I've only just started treating the wound. Come in and take a look at him if you like. Actually, do you mind waiting a moment while I change his dressing?'

Lucius followed her through the outer door. Through the bars of the cage, he saw the rear end of the tiger protruding from a wooden shelter. It had orange fur with black stripes, except for the tail, which was black and white, and flicked weakly.

Isidora took a roll of linen bandage and a small clay pot from a shelf near the outer door. The saliva dried in Lucius's mouth as he watched her pass through the inner door into the tiger's cage.

'You're not wearing any protection,' he croaked. It was an unwritten rule followed by everyone at the vivarium that you always put leather coverings on your arms and legs before coming into contact with a dangerous animal.

'They restrict my movements,' said Isidora.

Lucius watched, heart in mouth, as she closed the cage door behind her and went down on her hands and knees. 'This is the only way he'll let me touch him,' she said. 'I have to behave like I'm another tiger.'

She began to crawl very slowly towards Kato, keeping her head bowed in a gesture of submission. Tentatively, she reached out and stroked his haunch. The tail flicked in surprise.

Lucius stepped back in fright as the muscles beneath the orange fur began to ripple like the fire he'd once seen surging down Mount Vesuvius. The hind limbs stretched taut and the powerful animal climbed with terrifying swiftness to his feet. His spine curved as flexibly as a snake's as he twisted around, and suddenly his enormous head appeared at the entrance to his shelter. Kato's white-furred chin, calm green eyes and wide face reminded Lucius of something noble and kingly, making him reflect that perhaps the Egyptian tradition of animal worship was not so strange after all. Then the tiger's mouth opened wide, revealing a vicious set of teeth, and the godlike creature was abruptly transformed into a merciless killer. He could have decapitated Isi then and there with one casual bite. But the frightening display was merely a yawn, and soon his mouth shrank to something more like a grin. A large pink tongue played across his teeth and he let out another low growl. Isidora didn't flinch. She kept her head low to the ground.

Lucius could see the tiger wasn't quite balanced. All of his front-body weight was on his right leg. A dirty bandage covered his left paw, which hung limply in the air. With admirable calm and dexterity, Isidora began undoing the knot at the top of the bandage before slowly unwinding it. Kato seemed content to let her do her work. He licked his lips, and his growl was almost like a deep purr. When she'd removed the old bandage, she peered underneath the paw. 'It's looking a little better today,' she said.

Lucius watched in fear and wonder as four long claws, like curved dagger blades, emerged from the paw. 'One swipe with those and you're dead meat, you know that?' he whispered.

Isidora uttered a nervous chuckle. 'You don't need to remind me!'

Still maintaining her submissive posture, she pulled out the stopper of the clay jar with her teeth, then dipped her finger into the clear, amber-coloured substance it contained. 'Honey,' she murmured. 'My mother used to swear by it as a healer of infected wounds.' She pressed her finger to the dark gash beneath Kato's paw. He flinched. His eyes widened and he slashed with his claws. Isidora jerked her hand back, but slightly too late. Lucius saw a line of red appear on the flesh between her thumb and forefinger.

'Get out!' he cried. 'Get out of there now!'

'No, it's OK,' insisted Isidora, quickly tearing off some cloth from the roll and winding it around her wounded hand. 'He's just reacting to the pain. He'll be fine now.'

Deftly, she wound some more of the cloth roll around his paw and secured it with a knot. This time,

Kato didn't resist. Within a few minutes Isidora was safely out of the cage.

'Are you sure you're OK?' Lucius asked her.

'Fine,' she reassured him. She raised the hem of her tunic and showed him a long, shallow scar on her thigh. 'That happened on my *first* visit to his cage,' she explained. 'It's just a matter of getting used to each other. He's learning about me, and I'm learning about him. This time was my fault. I was probably a bit too forceful, and then too slow in getting out of the way.'

A loud shriek from further along the aisle made them both look up. A chimpanzee went bounding past them, nearly knocking Lucius over as it went.

'Don't just stand there!' bellowed Silus, coming up fast behind it and brandishing his bullwhip. 'Stop that blasted monkey!'

Obediently, Lucius began chasing the chimp down the long aisle. It lolloped along on all fours in its ungainly style, frequently looking back over its shoulder as it ran, baring its teeth and screeching, as if daring Lucius to catch it. There seemed little hope of that. It leapt at the bars of the antelope enclosure and clambered upwards with astonishing agility. Then it stood up on the roof of the enclosure, puffed out its chest, raised its long arms and hooted at Lucius, making the boy feel as if he was being cursed and mocked and jeered all at the same time.

'Get him down!' grunted the breathless Silus when he caught up with him. 'I want that monkey now, d'you hear? I'm going to flay him alive and then chop off his head and feed his brains to the hyenas. I'm going to use his skull as a soup bowl. Look at this!'

He held up his left hand. The bite mark showed clearly in the flesh of his palm. 'I was giving the wretched thing a well-deserved beating and this is what he did to me. Then he scarpered through the open door of the cage.' He raised his eyes to the chimp, which was now scampering manically about on the roof of the cage, still yelling and hooting at them. 'You may well laugh now, you hairy little demon, but you'll be crying for mercy by the time I'm finished with you!'

'Why did you beat him?' Isidora wanted to know.

'What sort of a question is that?' Silus snarled, his eyes narrowing dangerously on her innocent-looking face. 'I don't need reasons to beat those in my charge – and that goes for slaves, by the way, as well as animals. I'll beat anyone who thinks they've got the better of old Silus. Tried to steal my whip, didn't he? – when my back was turned. Steal it right out of my belt. And he very nearly succeeded! But old Silus was too quick for him!' He raised his head and repeated this to the chimp at the top of his voice: 'Too quick for you, wasn't I, you hairy gorgon?'* Returning his attention to Isidora, he added: 'I caught the whip with one hand and grabbed the monkey by the scruff of the neck with the other. Then I beat him soundly... No less

---

* *gorgon: a mythical monster: a woman with snakes for hair. Anyone who sees her face is turned to stone.*

than you deserved!' he bawled at the chimp. 'And I'd have carried on beating him for a good while longer if he hadn't suddenly leapt up and sunk his banana-chompers into me.'

Isidora tried to stifle her giggles behind her hand, but Silus spotted this and turned on her menacingly with his bullwhip. 'Back to your duties, girl, if you don't want to feel the sting of this crop across your hide.' She moved away, but only as far as a small crowd of fellow workers who had gathered in the aisle – this kind of entertainment was too rare to miss out on.

'What are *you* standing there gaping at?' Silus yelled at Lucius. 'Fetch a ladder from the storeroom and get him down from that roof.'

Five minutes later, Lucius was making his way unsteadily up a rickety ladder, to the sniggers of the watching crowd. The chimp grew ever more noisy and agitated the closer he came. When he reached the roof, Lucius stretched out and tried to grab the animal's leg. The chimp leapt clear and howled its indignation, then took off across the roof of the cage in the same quick, lolloping style, using its long arms just like another pair of legs.

'Get after him!' screamed Silus, and Lucius did. When the chimp sprang nimbly across a gap three paces wide to land on the roof of the next cage, Lucius gasped and slowed, but was soon roused by distant threats of violence from Silus if he didn't get a move on. Taking a deep breath, he sprinted across the rest of the roof and took off into space. For a second he was flying, to the gasps of the watchers below. Then, to his huge relief, he felt the impact of the next cage roof reverberating through the soles of his sandals. He'd made it! But he'd landed closer to the edge than he realised, and a small stumble backwards nearly sent him toppling to his doom. Desperately he windmilled his arms to try and regain his balance.

He managed it – just – and took off once again after his quarry. The hairy little figure had, by now, leapt another gap. Lucius gulped and followed him with another run and leap, this time landing more deftly. But the chimp, it seemed, was always one gap ahead, and by the time Lucius had vaulted a third aisle, the animal was scrambling up the stone outer wall of the vivarium.

Within seconds the chimp had reached the top. He stood tall there for a moment, beating his chest triumphantly and making cacophanous whoops at Lucius, before swiftly disappearing over the far side.

'Where's he gone?' a breathless Silus demanded from below, white spit now flecking his beard.

'He's escaped over the wall,' Lucius gasped.

'The outer wall?'

Lucius grimaced and nodded. The ape was now running free through the city streets.

CHAPTER II

1 MARCH

Lucius hurtled through the gates of the vivarium, Silus's final threat still ringing in his ears: 'Bring him back before nightfall, boy, or I'll have your skin for shoe leather.' Somehow, the chimp's escape had become, over the past quarter of an hour, entirely Lucius's fault – Lucius's responsibility. Silus had conveniently forgotten his own stupidity in letting the animal escape from its cage in the first place.

Stifling his anger, Lucius scanned the busy street, trying to catch a glimpse of the cheeky little ape. A fruit seller was leading a donkey along the cobbles, its back bent with the weight of the baskets it was carrying, filled with figs and apricots.

'Have you seen a chimpanzee?' Lucius asked.

'A what?'

'Never mind.'

The street was a swirl of activity. An acrobat was turning somersaults for the entertainment of a crowd waiting to buy hot sausages from a street vendor. Beggar children were clutching at the tunics of passing pedestrians.

'Can you spare a copper?' a child asked Lucius. Her feet were wrapped in rags.

Lucius handed her a coin. 'Have you seen a – ?'

He never completed the sentence, for just then he glimpsed the blur of a furry little body, flashing down an intersecting street in the direction of the river. Lucius charged after it, nearly knocking over a public-notice writer on a ladder as he went.

He chased the dark, scampering figure down a narrow street lined with warehouse buildings and poor fishermen's dwellings. At the far end, he came to the busy Via Aurelia, bustling with wagons carrying cargo to and from the river. He could see the chimp nipping between the legs of pedestrians, causing several to trip. Children laughed and pointed as the animal leapt onto a fisherman's stall, grabbed an eel and took a bite from its flesh, before disappearing into the road. A horse whinnied and a cart skidded to a halt. Briefly, the chimp could be seen clutching the mane of a horse like a mad charioteer from the Circus Maximus.* Then it slid off and was gone once again.

* *Circus Maximus: the great stadium where chariot races were held.*

Lucius caught his breath and continued the chase, pushing his way through the crowds to arrive, finally, at the greeny-brown waters of the Tiber. The view to his left was dominated by Tiber Island, the islet in the middle of the river where old or sick slaves lived out their remaining days after being abandoned by their masters. In his worst nightmares, he'd had visions of ending up there. Lucius wasn't a slave, of course, though he often felt like one these days.

The chimp, he noticed, was already bounding up the ramp of the Pons Aemilius,* the bridge leading to the centre of Rome. Lucius sighed – the animal was always just out of reach.

On the far side of the bridge lay the Portus Tiberinus, the main port of Rome. Wooden jetties jutted into the dirty river. Dockers swarmed over the jetties and the vessels moored there, loading and unloading large crates, some of which might contain more animals destined for the vivarium.

As he stood there on the quayside trying to see where the chimp had got to, Lucius was startled by a sudden rhythmic banging. A line of priests was emerging from the nearby temple to Portunus, a god of harbours and warehouses. They were striking blunt swords against their shields, making a deafening racket as they marched along the bank of the Tiber.

* *Pons Aemilius: this bridge crossed the River Tiber near the eastern tip of the Insula Tiberina (Tiber Island). Only one arch of the bridge is still standing today, and it is known in Italian as Ponte Rotto (broken bridge).*

Lucius wasn't the only one to be startled – the chimp suddenly leapt up from where it had been hiding beneath a jetty, right in front of the leader of the procession, and began shrieking its displeasure. The priest jumped back in fright, knocking the man behind him, who lost his balance and fell into the river. The man surfaced immediately, spluttering and yelling, to the amused guffaws of the watching dockers and fishermen.

For Lucius, the chase was on again. He dashed after the chimp into the Forum Boarium, the city's meat and fish market, which lay behind the docks. It was getting on towards lunchtime and the large cobbled square was crowded with customers and stallholders with their pink, gleaming produce laid out in trays before them. In the distance, Lucius could see cattle traders leading their animals into pens – the forum doubled as a livestock market. Weaving through the crowds were beggars, snake charmers, jugglers and touts selling tickets for the forthcoming Inaugural Games. It was a noisy, sweaty crush, and the air was thick with the salty smells of fresh carcasses and animal dung.

Lucius's shoulders slumped in despair as he watched his quarry vanish into the mêlée, knowing that there was now almost no chance of finding the chimp. Weary and anxious, he turned around, already mentally preparing himself for the wrath of Silus. The loss of a single chimpanzee meant little in the great scheme of things – but if news of its escape should happen to reach the ears of the city's praetor,* it could spell trouble for Silus – he might even lose his licence.

Occupied as he was with fears of how Silus might react, Lucius almost failed to see a dog sitting directly in his path. The dog barked just as Lucius was about to walk right into it. He jerked to a halt and glanced down. The glance turned into a stare of confusion, amazement – and finally joy, as he recognised the large, brown-eyed dog gazing back at him.

'Argos!' cried Lucius, falling to his knees and embracing his beloved, long-lost pet. He relished the familiar musky odour and the feel of warm, soft fur against his cheek. Argos whined and panted and nuzzled Lucius.

'Oh, Argos, where have you been? What happened to you?'

The dog had gone missing on the day the soldiers came to arrest Lucius's father, eight long months ago. Once or twice since then Lucius thought he'd glimpsed him in the crowded streets, but could never be sure. He'd really started to believe that Argos was gone forever.

'Look at you!' he said, examining the dog's lustrous brown fur and strong, healthy body. 'Someone's been looking after you. You've found a new master, haven't you? Admit it!'

'Woof!' replied Argos, wagging his tail. He began trotting away, heading towards the northern end of

* praetor: a senior official elected by the Senate.

the forum. He looked back and whined when Lucius hesitated to follow him.

'I have to get back to work, boy,' Lucius explained. 'Why don't you come with me?' He started back towards the dockside.

The dog whined again and didn't move.

Lucius stopped and frowned. 'Oh well, I suppose I *am* still officially looking for the chimp.' He shrugged and began following Argos through the square.

Beyond the Forum Boarium, they entered the bustling streets of the Velabrum, where, according to tradition, the roots of a fig tree once caught and stopped a basket floating along the Tiber current; the basket was carrying the infant twins Romulus and Remus, the legendary founders of Rome. Today, the Velabrum was a busy, industrious quarter, its streets full of oil and wine emporia, bakeries and sellers of herbs and spices. To their right loomed the steep brown sides of the Palatine Hill, capped with pillared temples and white Senatorial mansions.

Lucius was jostled to one side by a phalanx of attendants carrying a wealthy man in his litter* returning from the nearby Forum Romanum – the great open space that was the centre of the city's public life. As a result, he nearly lost sight of Argos, but then spotted him again as he turned into a narrow side street. He followed the dog through the dim entrance of an

* litter: a bed or chair carried on poles.

insula.* He could hear the echoing splashes and shouts from a cheap bathhouse across the street. An acrid smell of urine wafted from a public tank in front of the building – placed there by the fullers, who used it for cleaning clothes.

Lucius's heart sank a little at the damp, crumbling plaster walls of the entrance corridor. The insulae were where Rome's ordinary people lived – the *plebs*, as they were known. Lucius's family now also lived in one, in Suburra, but it was, at least, solidly constructed – unlike this place. So this was where Argos had ended up – his poor dog had fared even worse than him. He hesitated near the entrance. Argos had one paw on the first step of a narrow, twisting flight of stairs.

'Argos, I can't come in here. You have a new master now.' He looked at the dog's sad, uncomprehending eyes. 'I'm sorry, but…' His throat tightened and he found he couldn't continue. He turned to go, pretending not to hear the dog's whining.

As he made his way back down the street, Lucius thought to himself: *It was lovely to see my dog again, and to know that he's still alive and cared for by someone, but I can't possibly take him back. It would be unfair to his new owner and, besides, where would I keep him? Our landlord doesn't allow pets.*

'Lucius, is it really you?' came a hesitant voice from behind him. He whirled around. Standing there at the

* *insula: an apartment building, with shops on the ground floor and flats above; the tallest of them were up to nine storeys high.*

entrance to the insula was his old tutor, Agathon. His spotless white tunic had been replaced by a grubby brown one. His neatly trimmed beard had become as overgrown as a wild olive bush, but there was no mistaking his round stub of a nose and the humorous, intelligent twinkle in his dark eyes.

'Agathon!'

Lucius ran to him and the two embraced. This was the first time, Lucius suddenly realised, that he had ever hugged his tutor. The idea would have seemed absurd in his former life – Agathon was a slave, and their difference in status would not have allowed it. Now it felt perfectly natural, which was a vivid illustration of how far Lucius had fallen.

'It is good to see you, Lucius,' said Agathon, standing back and drinking in the sight of his former pupil. 'I felt sure that one day Argos would find you and lead you here and we would meet again.'

Agathon massaged the dog's neck fur with his slim, pale hand.

'So Argos is yours now?' gasped Lucius. 'That's… that's wonderful. I couldn't have wished him a better master.'

'Thank you. It happened by accident. Within a day of our departure from your father's villa, Ravilla sold me to a wealthy wine merchant who wanted a tutor for his son. But the son took a dislike to my teaching methods, and the merchant, having no more use for me, offered me my freedom. I found Argos soon afterwards, begging for scraps with all the other strays in the meat and fish market.'

'So, you're a freedman!' exclaimed Lucius. 'Congratulations!'

'Much good it has done me!' Agathon shrugged. 'Now I work in a scriptorium, laboriously copying out books on history and philosophy until my head aches, and for this I earn barely enough to pay the rent on a delapidated fourth-floor fire hazard here in the Velabrum. I must use street fountains for water, and my bathroom is the public latrine. If I am honest, my heart yearns for my slave days in your father's beautiful villa. But enough about me – I am desperate to hear your news. I have an hour before I must be back at work. Come, let us go out and get some lunch. I know an excellent popina nearby where they do a filling stew for just one sestertius,* and without a trace of dog meat in it – or so they assure me.'

Lucius and Agathon spent an enjoyable half-hour crouched around a tiny table in the crowded popina, exchanging news and recounting treasured memories of their former lives together. Meanwhile, Argos lay contentedly under the table, gnawing on an ox bone that Agathon had purchased cheaply from the butcher next door. Although Lucius tried to keep the talk light and to focus on recent events, the memory of his father haunted their conversation.

* *popina: a cheap bar selling wine and simple food; sestertius: a brass coin, worth one hundredth of a golden aureus.*

Towards the end of the meal, Agathon grew solemn. 'I have something for you, Lucius,' he said. 'I have been keeping it safely in the hope that one day we would meet again.'

'What is it?' cried Lucius, suddenly on fire with curiosity.

Agathon checked over both shoulders to make sure he wasn't being overheard, then leaned in close. 'About eight weeks ago, I received a letter from your father.'

Lucius's heart skipped several beats.

He'd last received word from his father seven months ago, through Rufus, the gladiator, who'd died before he could arrange a meeting between them. Since then there had been complete silence, during which time Lucius had almost given up hope. In his bleakest moments, he imagined his father dead – secretly killed by Ravilla's agents. Lucius had tried to steel himself to the prospect of never seeing his father again, and had almost convinced himself that he no longer missed him. Yet this news of Agathon's brought an immediate and powerful surge of emotion. He felt hot tears springing to his eyes, and almost heard a crack in the hard layers of ice that had accumulated inside his chest.

'Where is the letter?' he asked thickly.

'It's in my apartment. We can go there now if you like.'

Agathon's apartment consisted of two small, simply furnished rooms – a bedroom, and a sitting room with a small desk and a couple of chairs. The thin walls admitted noises from neighbours – crying infants, shouts and snores. From the street below came the creak of cart wheels, dogs barking and the cries of hawkers. These sounds barely registered for Lucius, however, as he watched Agathon hunt around inside a chest in his bedroom.

Eventually he found the parchment scroll and handed it to Lucius. Before he began reading, Lucius allowed himself a moment to enjoy the calm, measured strokes of his father's handwriting. It gave him a sense of peace and serenity he hadn't felt in a long time. The letter, according to the date, was recent – just eight weeks old. His father still lived! And this was not the desperate scrawl of someone close to the end, but the relaxed and deliberate penmanship of a man who still believed that fate was on his side. Lucius began to read:

Quintus Valerius Aquila sends greetings to Aemilius Paullus Agathon.

I hope this letter finds you well, my old friend. You are often in my thoughts, and it was a great pleasure to hear, through a contact, of your recent manumission.* This is well deserved, and I am only sorry that it was not I who was able to grant your freedom to you. I trust that you are still teaching and that you have found a post worthy of your talents.

* *manumission: setting free from slavery.*

As you know, my circumstances these past six months have not been easy. My freedom of movement is severely curtailed and I must change my abode constantly to evade my enemies who lie in wait for me, ready to pounce should I make even the briefest appearance in a public place. I am therefore forced to rely on the goodwill of friends and family to assist me in my current plight and help me achieve the restoration of my good name.

I trust I can count you, Agathon, among my friends, and I beg, as a friend, for your assistance in a crucial and highly sensitive matter. My hopes of achieving justice depend on my ability to present written proof of my innocence. It so happens that written proof exists, and I must get hold of this urgently. The proof takes the form of a letter to my brother Ravilla from the late emperor Vespasian. It confirms that Ravilla is the Spectre, not I. My trusted associates assure me of the existence of this letter and that it is hidden somewhere in Ravilla's house.

I am familiar enough with my brother's prideful, scheming nature to know that he will not have destroyed this letter. He firmly believes that Titus will not be emperor for long, and the time will shortly come when Titus's brother Domitian will take the purple.* Domitian, being possessed of a character even more power-hungry, cynical and paranoid than his father's, will almost certainly have a need for informers; Ravilla is therefore confident that his time will come again. This is why he will not have destroyed the letter – for he will need it to prove to Domitian that he was Vespasian's most feared informer.

* *take the purple: become emperor. Purple dye was expensive and purple clothes were worn only by the nobility.*

I need to prove the very same thing – but to Titus. I would not ask you to steal the letter, Agathon, nor to hire a professional housebreaker to do so. Ravilla's house is too well guarded, and any attempt to break in will only encourage him to redouble his security. We must approach this task more subtly, without alerting my brother to our purpose. We need Ravilla to welcome the thief into his home. You were always quick-witted, Agathon, and I am sure that you will have already guessed the direction of my thinking...

I need you to find Lucius for me. Of all my family, my younger son is temperamentally the best suited to this task. The boy must find some excuse to visit Ravilla's house, or else contrive to get himself invited there. And while there, he must steal the letter.

As to where he might find it, I remember that when my brother was a young man, he owned a small, red, lockable box where he kept all his most treasured secrets. I am certain that the letter, if it is anywhere, will be in that box, and that the box is somewhere in his bedroom.

You now know what I need from you, Agathon. I pray to the gods that you are able to carry out this request. Please show this message to Lucius when you find him, then destroy it.

I will write again in due course to let you know where to send Vespasian's letter. Thank you, my friend. I am exceedingly obliged to you.

Aquila

Lucius continued staring at the letter for a long time

after he'd finished reading it. He felt proud that his father had selected him for this vital task. At the same time, he shuddered at the challenge facing him.

He let Agathon remove the letter from his fingers and hold it over the flame of an oil lamp. As he watched the corner of the parchment catch light, part of him wanted to snatch it back – apart from the chalcedony ring, handed to him by Rufus, which he always wore on his finger, it was his only link to his father. But he understood that the letter had to be destroyed – it was far too risky to keep.

Soon enough, the parchment was just ashes, which Agathon swept into his modest hearth.

'It seems like an impossible task,' said Lucius despondently. 'First of all, how am I going to get Ravilla to invite me to his house? And even if I manage that, how will I be able to get away from him for long enough to slip into his bedroom and find this box? And what if it's locked? I'll have to steal it, so we can break into it later. How could I ever sneak something like that out of the house?' His head sank as the extreme danger and difficulty of the mission became apparent to him.

'I don't know the answers to any of these questions,' said Agathon gently. 'But I am confident that you will find a way. Just think how much is at stake. If you can get your hands on this one letter, you will have the means to save not only your father, but also yourself and the rest of your family. All that your family has lost shall be restored to you. If there is any justice in this world, that is what will happen.'

Lucius looked up at Agathon's sad, kindly face. 'If it happens,' he smiled, 'then I swear by Minerva, goddess of wisdom, that my first act will be to ask my father to take you back as our tutor – but this time as a freedman!'

Argos barked cheerfully, sensing a brightening of the mood.

'And we'll have *you* back as well, of course, my beauty!' added Lucius.

Agathon laughed and clapped Lucius on the shoulder. 'One thing at a time, Lucius. First, steal that letter!'

'You've got a nerve,' Silus yelled at Lucius on his return to the vivarium. 'Where've you been all this time? How could you let that hairy imp slip through your fingers?' He glared at Lucius suspiciously. 'I don't believe you even tried catching him, did you? The minute you were out of those gates, you were off down the tavern playing knucklebones with the local layabouts. Well, I'll tell you now, this is all your fault, boy. If it gets back to the praetor that one of my animals is loose in this city, I'm going to have your hair for helmet plumes and your gnashers for necklace beads – understand? Now get down to the bull enclosure and help that useless girlfriend of yours clean the stables. There's about thirty days' worth of dung in there that needs clearing.'

Lucius went off without a word. He'd learnt long ago that there was no point in arguing with Silus – unless you wanted to get whipped. Besides, he was pleased to have an opportunity to talk in private with Isidora.

He found her amidst about half a dozen bulls, up to her knees in straw and muck, pitchfork in hand, loading heaps of the soiled bedding into a wheelbarrow. When she saw Lucius, she wiped her forehead with the back of her hand.

'Well, Silus hasn't skinned you alive, so I guess you must have found the chimp.'

Lucius shook his head. 'I couldn't find him anywhere.'

'That's great!' she laughed. 'I hope he ends up as a senator's pet, living it up on the Palatine Hill. They should build a statue to him – the greatest escape artist since Icarus.'*

'I hope so too. Then I'll be in the clear. All Silus really cares about is that the praetor doesn't get to hear about this. If he does, I really will be dead meat.'

'I doubt it,' said Isidora. 'I know Silus enjoys threatening people, but he wouldn't dare hurt the

---

* *Icarus: in Greek mythology, the son of the inventor Daedalus. Both escaped from imprisonment on the island of Crete by using wings made by Daedalus, but Icarus flew too close to the sun and his wings melted.*

nephew of Ravilla – not unless Ravilla wants him to, of course.'

Lucius picked up a shovel and began shifting dung. 'Speaking of Ravilla, something happened to me just now, while I was searching for the chimpanzee.'

'Oh?' Isidora looked up, her eyes suddenly bright with interest.

He checked over his shoulder to make sure they were alone. 'I met a couple of old friends…'

He told her what had happened, including the letter from his father and what he had been asked to do.

'I know all about Ravilla's red box!' interrupted Isidora when he got to that part. 'Remember I used to be a slave in his house? He keeps it in a big chest at the foot of his bed.' She frowned for a moment, deep in thought. Then she looked up. 'Maybe we can do this together!'

'Together? No offence, Isi, but there's no way my uncle would ever invite *you* to his house…'

'I don't mean that… Look, while you're there, you can find some excuse to get away from the dinner, then sneak into his bedroom and open a window. Then I can climb in and steal the red box.'

'But how will you get inside his property?' asked Lucius. 'It's very well guarded.'

'Oh, don't worry about that,' said Isidora carelessly. 'I'm like a cat. No one'll see me!'

'He may have a dog,' said Lucius. 'And dogs *love* chasing cats.'

Isidora didn't seem remotely fazed by this possibility. 'Listen,' she said, 'if I can handle a tiger, I don't think a dog is going to give me too much trouble.'

CHAPTER III

Suburra, the neighbourhood where Lucius lived with his mother and sister, was the poorest, roughest part of Rome. The vagrants here were even more ragged and had fewer teeth than those in the Velabrum. Pickpockets haunted the market squares, and thieves and tomb robbers swapped tales of villainy in the taverns. A coin dropped into a hat by a passing nobleman could spark a vicious fight between rival beggars. The nights often rang to the sounds of violent scuffles and screams, and it was not uncommon to find corpses lying in the streets, come the dawn.

Lucius did not relish his walk home each evening. As the sun began to sink and the shadows lengthened across the city, Suburra's streets took on a menacing aspect, the way a mischievous grin can, in altered light, turn into a sinister leer. From an alleyway, he heard a howl of anguish, followed by peals of childish laughter. Peering into the gloom, he glimpsed a gang of boys surrounding some unfortunate passer-by, throwing pebbles and rotten fruit at the unseen victim. The oldest looked no more than ten. Even so, Lucius was hesitant to get involved. In Suburra, he'd seen younger kids than these carrying knives.

The victim emitted another guttural shriek of pain. The sound was strange – almost inhuman. Behind Lucius, a jeweller pulled down the shutter of his shop, as if wishing to block out this disturbing noise.

Despite his fear, Lucius took a step closer to the alleyway. He saw that it ended in a brick wall. The victim was trapped and the boys were closing in, laughing and throwing anything they could lay their hands on – shards of broken amphorae,* bones discarded by butchers, carpenters' nails. The projectiles bounced and clinked against the cobbles. The victim leapt onto a withered vine growing up the rear wall of the alley and tried to climb it. Something about the small, shadowy figure and its lithe, graceful movements seemed familiar to Lucius.

The chimpanzee!

A branch cracked, and the chimp went tumbling back into the alley. Its howl sounded close to despair.

* *amphorae: pottery storage jars.*

Lucius's fear was now eclipsed by fury that these children should choose to torment an innocent animal. He ran into their midst and roughly pushed one of them aside before he could launch another missile.

'Leave it alone!' he shouted at them.

The bullies stared up at him, momentary surprise quickly turning to impish amusement. They were, he now saw, no more than bored street urchins, some of them as young as six. Scaring the chimp was just a way of passing the time.

'Get away from here,' said Lucius, speaking more softly. 'Go back to your homes.' Even as he said it, he wondered if any of them *had* homes. But the boys wandered away, nudging each other and giggling as they went.

Lucius felt the breath of the chimp close by, and a rough, long-fingered hand closed around his. He looked down. The chimp bared its teeth and made a low, breathy, grunting sound. Lucius was startled at first, but then a warm feeling spread through his chest. The chimp's deep brown eyes explored his, searching for what? Compassion? Forgiveness?

'You need protecting, my little friend,' said Lucius gently. 'These streets are not for you. Come with me.' He began leading the chimp home. Tomorrow, he supposed, he would have to take it back to the vivarium. He prayed Silus would not to be too hard on the poor creature.

Home for Lucius was a first-floor apartment in the

heart of the Suburra slums. The ground floor of the insula was taken up by the workshops of weavers, potters and metalworkers, selling cheap household goods. Positioned directly under his family's apartment was a fast-food outlet. Oil lamps dangling from the base of their apartment balcony illuminated the big, swinging sign – CALVA'S THERMOPOLIUM* – and the faces of hungry customers, lining up before the counter. Serving them their hot sausages, cheese, dates and warm wine was the fat, smiling owner, Antigonus Calva.

Lucius had noticed that Calva, although outwardly friendly, had a sly, ruthless streak. He'd had his eye on the apartment above his shop for years as a home for his girlfriend, and was annoyed when Lucius's family had moved in. Since then he had been looking for any excuse to be rid of them. If he knew that Lucius was trying to sneak a wild animal in there, Calva would go straight to the owner of the insula and report him. Lucius was therefore careful to keep to the shadows as he led the chimp through the narrow entrance beside Calva's shop that would take him up to their apartment.

The apartment was only slightly bigger than Agathon's. Besides the sitting room and its tiny, adjoining kitchen, there were two small bedrooms – one shared by Lucius's mother Caecilia and his sister Valeria, the other occupied by Lucius. He had briefly shared it with his older brother Quintus, until Quin

* *thermopolium: Greek for 'hot food shop'.*

moved out just over seven months ago to go and live with his new familia at the gladiator school. Quin's bed was still there in one corner, in case he should ever decide to return, but Lucius doubted he ever would.

When Lucius came in, Caecilia was spinning yarn by the window. Eleven-year-old Valeria was seated on the floor by the room's single oil lamp, practising her writing on a wax tablet. Mother's and daughter's hands were red from their long days spent cleaning and repairing gladiators' uniforms. As the chimp came shambling in behind Lucius, both jumped back in surprise.

'Lucius! What have you brought?' cried Caecilia, dropping her spindle and pressing herself close against the wall.

'It's a monkey!' laughed Valeria, clapping her hands in delight.

'A chimpanzee,' corrected Lucius. He turned to Caecilia. 'Don't worry, mother. I shall take him back to the vivarium tomorrow. He escaped from there today, and luckily I found him on my way home. He'll be no trouble, I promise.'

As he was saying this, the chimp was moving in his clumsy way around the room, picking up objects, examining them and then tossing them over his shoulder when he realised they weren't food. Lucius, running behind him, managed to catch a Lar statuette – one of the precious guardian deities of their home – before it smashed on the floor, but was too late to intercept a water jug and a jar of face powder, both of which shattered into fragments. The chimp gave a screech as he caught sight of his face in a polished bronze hand mirror, and began jumping up and down excitedly.

'Get that thing out of here at once!' exclaimed Caecilia. 'It's going to break everything.'

'No, mamma!' pleaded Valeria, running to the chimp and throwing her arms protectively around him. 'He's just exploring, that's all. I think he's wonderful. We must keep him. Lucius, you mustn't take him back to the nasty vivarium tomorrow. He escaped because he hated it there. Didn't you, my little pet?'

Lucius and Caecilia watched, amazed, as the chimpanzee immediately grew calmer in Valeria's embrace. He stared at her as if at a long-lost friend.

'You're hungry, aren't you, little one?' she said to him. 'Come with me. I have some dates in my bedroom.' The chimp reached out one of his long arms and grasped her hand, then Valeria escorted him out of the room.

'You can't keep that creature, Val,' called Caecilia. 'It can stay for tonight, but Lucius is taking it back tomorrow morning. Tomorrow morning, you hear?'

Valeria didn't reply. From the other room, they could hear her speaking softly and sweetly to her new friend.

Lucius wanted to tell Caecilia his news about Argos, Agathon and the letter from his father, but he was hesitant. They rarely talked of Aquila these days. What was the point? She was so certain of his guilt, and Lucius was so convinced of his innocence, it was as if they were speaking about two different people. Many times he'd been on the point of telling her about what he'd learned in Pompeii – that Ravilla, not Aquila, was the Spectre – but he'd always decided against it. She was so stubborn in her opinions, and as he couldn't provide any proof, he was sure she'd never believe him. If he told her, it would only create further tension between them.

But what he'd learnt today was different. This information had come directly from Aquila, and for the first time there was something practical that Lucius could do to help his father. He decided it was important to tell his mother about Aquila's letter, even if she disapproved.

'Mother,' he began, 'you'll never believe it – I found Argos today in the meat market…'

Caecilia listened to the whole story without reacting or interrupting. When he had finished, she leaned back in her chair and continued with her spinning. With her face half in shadow, Lucius couldn't easily see her expression. Laughter drifted up from the street below. On the building opposite were adverts for the Inaugural Games painted in large red letters that flickered in the light from Calva's oil lamps.

'What do you think, Mother?' Lucius prompted. 'This is good news, isn't it?'

She put down her spindle and looked up. Her face was pale and hard as marble. 'Your father must be dreaming if he thinks Ravilla is the Spectre,' she said quietly. 'Of course he isn't. These claims he is now making are a sign of his desperation. Forget him, Lucius. Aquila is nothing to us now. We belong to Ravilla.'

Lucius stared at her, shocked. He should have expected this, of course – he knew her views. But the words, spoken with such coldness, still took his breath away. 'You're talking about my father,' he said. 'The man you married. How can you just dismiss this letter like the words of a delinquent slave?'

'You think it's easy?' said Caecilia, as spots of angry colour bloomed in her cheeks. 'You think a day goes by when I don't miss my former life? But I've accepted that that life is over. And so should you, Lucius! Aquila is not the man I thought I'd married. He lied to me, as he lied to everyone, including you! Don't be fooled – he *was* the Spectre! And now he's trying to pin the blame on his brother – and even involving *you* in his hopeless schemes. This I cannot forgive. If he had any honour, any decency, he would tell you to forget about him.'

For Lucius, these words were pure torture. The gulf between him and his mother was so enormous, he didn't think it could ever be bridged. What would it take to convince her?

The sound, close by, of stifled sobbing startled him.

He turned to see his sister standing in the doorway of her bedroom, sniffing back tears. He hadn't realised she'd been listening.

Caecilia got up and went to embrace her.

'I hate it when you say those things about Father,' wept Valeria.

'Go to bed, dear,' murmured Caecilia. 'We'll talk about it in the morning.'

'Can the chimpanzee sleep in our room, Mother?' Valeria asked.

'No,' said Caecilia firmly. 'I'm not having that filthy thing in our bedroom. It can stay with Lucius.'

'Well, can I at least keep him here until you come to bed?'

'All right,' Caecilia agreed wearily.

When his mother returned to the living room, Lucius said softly: 'In Pompeii, I heard Ravilla confess to being the Spectre.'

Caecilia sighed as she settled herself back into her seat by the window. 'What are you talking about?' she said.

Lucius told her about the meeting he'd overheard between Valens and Ravilla, but before he'd even finished the story she was already shaking her head.

'I've heard tales of this Valens character,' said Caecilia. 'Some of the gladiators who come into the fullery to get their uniforms cleaned are refugees from Pompeii. They say Valens was as slippery as a sewer rat. He would fabricate evidence against anyone if he thought it would make him some money. I'm sure he viewed Ravilla, a high-ranking senator from Rome, as easy meat. If Ravilla admitted to anything it was probably only to buy himself time. Of course he didn't mean it. He was pretending to fall into Valens's trap, while planning to deal with him later. Luckily, the mountain took care of the problem for him.'

'It wasn't like that,' Lucius protested – but he knew he was wasting his breath. His mother had closed her mind to any possibility that Ravilla might be guilty. As far as she was concerned, the matter was settled.

'Remember who your friends are, Lucius,' Caecilia warned. 'Ravilla has been very good to us since Aquila's treachery was exposed. Without your uncle's help and protection, we might well have ended up in exile ourselves – or worse! You may think you're helping Aquila, but all you're doing is endangering your life – and all our lives. I beg you with all my heart to forget your father, ignore his letter, and desist from these dangerous games.'

Later, as Lucius was getting into bed, there came a soft tap on his door and Valeria entered, hand in hand with her now devoted companion, the chimpanzee.

'He's called Simio,' she said.

Lucius sighed. 'You shouldn't have given him a name, Val. You heard Mother. He's going back to the vivarium tomorrow and you'll never see him again.'

'It's all right, I have a plan,' said Valeria. 'My friend Euphemia across the street – her father breeds monkeys and other small creatures.'

'You mean Gordianus the tailor? He breeds animals?'

'Yes. He has a wild-animal enclosure.'

'In his apartment?!'

'No, silly! In a courtyard behind their insula. I've seen it! Anyway, Euphemia told me that her father's always on the lookout for animals that can do tricks. He rents them out to street performers. And I just know Simio will be brilliant at tricks. Look!'

Valeria tossed a ball at the chimp and he effortlessly plucked it out of the air and lobbed it back at her.

'See? And I haven't even started training him yet. Maybe once we've worked up a few routines, Mother will let me take him to the Forum. I could earn a lot more money there than I do at the fullery.'

Lucius bristled at the thought of his sister earning money as a street performer. The family hadn't sunk *that* low – not yet, anyway. 'Remember who you are, Valeria Prima Aquila,' he said to her.

She shrugged. 'It's just a name, Lucius. Mother's right about one thing at least: our old life is over. Now we must do whatever it takes to survive… I'm going to speak to Euphemia tomorrow. If she agrees, then Simio can stay with the other animals in the courtyard, and in the evenings I'll go over there and teach him some tricks.'

Lucius shook his head, but in amazement rather than disagreement. His little sister had grown up so fast. Perhaps this was what poverty did – it cut short childhood. She had formed a plan – a good one, too! And if Caecilia agreed to it, Simio the chimp would be able to start a new life safely out of Silus's reach.

'I'll help you persuade Mother,' he said to her.

A smile of joy spread across her face. 'Thank you, Lucius.' Then she turned and gazed proudly at Simio, who had become captivated by a boar's-tusk comb that he'd found, running his finger back and forth along the prongs. 'I'm so happy you brought him home,' breathed Valeria. 'He's absolutely the best thing that's happened to me since we moved here.'

Lucius noticed her chin wobble as she said this, and guessed she wasn't quite as content as she was claiming. Something was bothering her, and he could guess what it was.

'I'm sorry you had to hear those things Mother said earlier,' he said, '– about Father.'

'It's all right,' she said, in a hollow, vacant voice. Then she suddenly turned to him and squeezed his hand, eyes alive with excitement. 'Lucius, I heard you talk about that letter from Father. Do you think it's true that Ravilla has a letter in his house proving he's the Spectre?'

Lucius nodded.

'Then you must go there,' she said emphatically. 'And I will come, too!'

'Now wait a minute…' began Lucius.

'Please let me come! Don't you see that if I'm there, there's much less chance that Ravilla will think anything suspicious is going on. He thinks I'm as simple and innocent as a newborn lamb.'

'Then he doesn't know you!' Lucius chuckled.

'Tell him I miss him, and that I'm disappointed he never comes and sees us any more. Tell him I insist on paying him a visit and you will escort me there. He'll fall for it, I know he will! And once we're there, I can distract him while you go off and find that letter.'

Lucius could see how Val's presence would allay Ravilla's suspicions. All the same, he felt uneasy about involving his sister in such a risky undertaking. What if Ravilla discovered their real purpose? He couldn't bear it if anything happened to Val.

She guessed what he was thinking. 'We have to do whatever it takes to help Father,' she told him. 'Mother and Quin won't lift a finger, and you can't do it all on your own. You need my help.'

'I won't be on my own,' said Lucius. He told her about Isidora's offer to retrieve the red box.

'That's even better!' said Valeria, clapping her hands. 'Then all you need do is go into his bedroom and open the window. You'll be back in no time. What can go wrong?'

Lucius frowned. The two girls seemed to think that stealing the letter was a simple matter. He wasn't so sure.

'All right,' he said finally, 'you can be part of this. But if Ravilla finds out what our real plan is, I'm going to swear to him you knew nothing about it, and you're not to deny it – understood?'

Valeria began to protest, but Lucius cut her off.

'Promise me!' he insisted.

'All right,' she shrugged. 'I'll pretend to be innocent if you really want, but it doesn't make any difference because I just know nothing will go wrong…'

CHAPTER IV

2 MARCH

An opportunity to speak with Ravilla came sooner than Lucius had dared to expect. The following morning, Silus sent him and Isidora to the new Flavian Amphitheatre* for a tour of the underground cages, to which the animals would be transferred in three days' time. Once the games began, these subterranean vaults would become Lucius's and Isidora's place of work, and they needed to familiarise themselves with this new environment.

Fortunately for Lucius, the amphitheatre was very close to the Ludus Romanus, the gladiator school

---

* *Flavian Amphitheatre: a huge arena for gladiatorial combat and other entertainments, built by the emperors of the Flavian dynasty: Vespasian, Titus and Domitian. Today it is usually called the Colosseum.*

69

where Ravilla had his office. Both buildings had been constructed at the base of the Esquiline Hill, on the grounds of the Emperor Nero's hated Golden House, long since demolished. Lucius decided he would visit the school, and try to see Ravilla, as soon as their underground tour was over.

Isidora was full of excitement about Kato, the injured tiger she was looking after. 'He was so much perkier this morning,' she told Lucius as they walked. 'The pus from his wound is clear and no longer smells bad. And he's ravenous, which is always a good sign.'

'What did Silus say?' asked Lucius.

'He's overjoyed, of course. Kato's the only tiger we have at Trans Tiberim, so now Silus is really keen to keep him alive. He's ordered me to put live piglets in his cage to build up his hunting skills in time for the games.'

'Did you remind him that he wanted to kill Kato a few days ago?'

Isidora laughed. 'I didn't dare!'

On their arrival at the amphitheatre, the sight of the brand-new, gleaming white stadium was somewhat marred by the smelly mob they found camped out on the square in front of it. These, they quickly realised, were the poorest of the city, who couldn't afford tickets to the games and hoped to find themselves among the limited number offered free entry on the opening day. Lucius and Isidora picked their way carefully through the village of hide tents, the groups of unshaven men drinking wine and playing dice, and the discarded free bread being fought over by flocks of scavenging birds.

They were greeted near the amphitheatre's main entrance by their tour guide, a former Bestiarius* named Ramio. He was a giant of a man with three parallel scars running down his cheek, which, he cheerfully boasted, had been inflicted by the claws of a she-wolf whose mate he'd just slain. Nowadays Ramio was chief beastmaster at the training school for Bestiarii, but Lucius got the feeling he missed his glory days in the amphitheatre. He led them through a smaller, concealed entrance and down a flight of steps into the Hypogeum, the system of dark, airless stone tunnels that lay beneath the amphitheatre. The only light was provided by torches set at intervals along the walls, and the smoke from these often made breathing difficult. The whole place echoed with the howls and thrashings of the animals already installed in their cages, adding to Lucius's unpleasant feeling of claustrophobia. *How much worse this will be,* he reflected, *when all the cages are full of animals maddened by the smell of blood emanating from the arena above their heads?*

The network of tunnels filled the entire oval space beneath the arena and the surrounding stands. Elevator shafts would lift the animals directly from their holding pens through hidden trapdoors into the arena. Thick pillars carved from solid travertine soared above them, supporting the stands. An upper tier of tunnels

* *Bestiarius: a person who fights wild animals in the amphitheatre.*

71

beneath the stands led to arched gateways set within the arena's perimeter wall, providing yet more entry points for the animals into the arena.

'How are you going to force the animals through these exits?' Isidora wanted to know. 'They'll be dazzled by the light and frightened by the noise from the crowd, won't they?'

Ramio grinned and plucked a torch from a wall bracket. 'We'll have slaves behind them with these!' he chuckled. 'And if they escape past the firebrands, there'll be a line of men following up with wooden shields that'll fill the whole width of the corridor.' He indicated a set of grooves in the walls. 'The shields lock into these, so there's no way through for your panicked antelope or bull. One way or another, he'll end up in the arena!'

'It's going to be hell down there,' predicted Isidora as they tucked into their lunch of hot chickpea soup and bread, bought from one of the vendors on the square.

'I know,' agreed Lucius. 'We'll just have to do what we can to keep the animals calm. At least they won't know what's about to happen to them.'

Once the games began, most of the animals' lives would be measurable in days. Virtually all of those that ventured into the arena would have to be dragged off it shortly afterwards as carcasses – slaughtered for the entertainment of the crowd by Parthian archers, Bestiarii, Venatores* or other animals. Lucius and Isidora both knew this, and the thought depressed them too much for words.

When they'd finished their meal, Lucius got up from the bench they'd been sitting on. 'Right,' he said. 'On with the mission. I'm going to see if I can speak to Ravilla.'

'I think I'll come with you to the school,' said Isidora, wiping her mouth with her sleeve. 'I might snatch a word with Faustina, if she's on her lunch break.' Faustina was a fellow slave and friend of Isidora's from her days working at the school.

Durio, the porter at the gladiator school, greeted them with the smile of an old friend. 'What a pleasant surprise. And what brings you two back here?'

'I've come to see my uncle, if he's around,' said Lucius.

'Rushed off his feet, what with the games starting in a few days – but yes, he's here! So is your brother. In fact, I believe he's in the training arena right now. His session is due to end in a few minutes, so this might be a good chance to say hello.'

Lucius hadn't expected he'd be able to speak to Quin, knowing how intense his brother's training

* *Venatores: hunters.*

regime was during these final days of preparation, but he welcomed the opportunity.

Durio turned his attention to Isidora. 'How are *you*, my little Nile Princess?' That was what he always called her.

While the two of them chatted, Lucius stepped through the vestibule into the school's atrium.* The smells of fresh sweat and sawdust instantly took him back to the days when he had worked here. From beyond an arched doorway at the far end, he could hear the clash of wooden practice weapons and the grunts of hard-fighting men. He stepped through the doorway onto a colonnaded terrace and looked out across the enormous open-air quadrangle around which the school had been built. Everywhere he looked, there were gladiators lifting weights, thrusting their weapons at wooden posts or straw men, or practice-fighting in pairs.

The seasoned gladiators were outnumbered by more recent arrivals – prisoners of war and natives of far-flung provinces, brought here to swell the numbers and provide easy kills at the forthcoming games. Lucius saw olive-skinned Arab nomads and fierce-looking Sarmatians from Central Asia being barked at by burly under-trainers. Other novices – blond Germans and tall Africans with dark, polished skin – were running around the perimeter of the quad with lead weights attached to their ankles, while under-trainers

---

* *atrium: an entrance hall, partly open to the sky.*

hurled wooden staves at them, forcing them to dodge. Crassus, the school's lanista, was prowling around, stopping now and then to bellow advice to a fighting pair: 'Surprise is everything! Vary your retreats. Never let your opponent see a pattern. Show nothing with the eyes... You! Parry close to the body, that's it!'

The oval training arena, complete with wooden benches, lay in the middle of the quad. Threading a careful route through the flying swords and staves, Lucius made his way over there. He found Quin, armed with the net and trident of a Retiarius, engaging with a youthful-looking Secutor.* Lucius took a seat on one of the benches and watched them fight. Neither gladiator was wearing armour, and both were naked except for their loincloths. The pair were in constant motion, circling each other, ducking and weaving to avoid the other's attacks, then suddenly lunging with their weapons, stopping just short of their opponent's flesh. It was like watching an elaborate dance, or a mock fight between two male antelopes. Their muscles gleamed in the bright sunlight as they whirled and darted around the sandy space. Quin looked a picture of health and fitness, and Lucius found it hard to believe that just seven months ago his brother had come within a hair's-breadth of death.

In fact, Quin's miraculous escape from Pompeii, as well as his victories there, had turned him into

---

* *Retiarius: fighter with net (rete) and trident; Secutor: a sword-fighter, the traditional opponent of a Retiarius; the name means 'chaser'.*

something of a legend, both at the school and among his growing army of fans. Shortly after his return to Rome, the stories began to circulate about how he'd been poisoned and then buried under a pile of rocks during the eruption at Pompeii, before somehow emerging unscathed. With each retelling, the tale had become further embellished. In some versions, he had physically died from the poisoning and had then been brought back to life by the kiss of a Pompeiian witch. According to others, Quin had been buried beneath the fiery surge that engulfed Pompeii, only to be reborn from the ashes like a human Phoenix.* In truth, Quin had escaped from Pompeii more than an hour before the city was destroyed. He hadn't died, and there was no witch.

Privately, Quin laughed at these tales. Yet he understood the value of a legend when it came to furthering one's career as a gladiator – if the crowd believed that the gods wanted him alive, they were less likely to call for his death, should he lose a bout in the arena. So he took care not to deny any of the stories being told around the city's taverns, and instead maintained a lofty silence about the whole affair. He had returned to the arena for the first time three weeks ago for the games celebrating the purifying festival of Lupercalia, and he had won all three of his fights. His growing army of supporters boasted: not only

---

* *Phoenix: in Greek mythology, a bird that is periodically consumed by fire and then reborn.*

can Quintus Felix survive a fire-spewing mountain, he's also the greatest gladiator ever to wield the net and trident.

After ten more minutes of sparring, the two young men stopped and clasped hands in friendship. Then Quin threw an arm around his partner's shoulder and led him over to where Lucius was sitting. 'Trebellius,' smiled Quin, 'meet my younger brother Lucius. He used to work at this school, looking after us gladiators. Now he looks after wild beasts, which is a promotion if you ask me.'

Quin laughed gleefully at his own joke. He was in an almost manic state of high spirits, as he always was in the build-up to a big fight, and his face shone with exuberance as much as it did with sweat.

Trebellius laughed along with him and clasped wrists with Lucius. 'You were in Pompeii, too, I understand,' he said, fixing Lucius with a pair of sparkling blue eyes. 'One day, you must tell me what really happened down there. I've heard so many stories, I don't know what to believe…'

'You'll get a different story from every person you ask,' chuckled Quin. 'But if you want the truth, Lucius was the real hero of Pompeii.' A tender, thoughtful look suddenly intruded on his smile. 'He saved my life.'

It was the first time Quin had ever said such a thing, and Lucius was struck dumb. His cheeks burned and he couldn't meet his brother's eyes, but inside he felt very warm and proud. It made him realise just how far the two of them had come since those awful arguments they'd had after their father's disappearance. Quin, like Caecilia, firmly believed in Aquila's guilt, and had gone so far as to renounce the family name of Valerius, styling himself simply Quintus Felix. Pompeii had brought the two brothers closer. Following the eruption, Quin learnt from others how Lucius had cared for him after he was poisoned and had never given up on him, even when he was buried alive. These stories of his brother's steadfastness had touched him deeply. Since then, they'd maintained an amiable truce, both agreeing never to mention the one issue that continued to divide them: the guilt or innocence of their father, Aquila.

A few minutes later, Trebellius left the arena to get washed and changed, but Quin seemed in a mood to linger.

'Trebellius is new here, right?' Lucius said conversationally.

Quin nodded as he massaged a sore muscle in his shoulder. 'He's from down south in Calabria originally – an expert fighter, and also one of the friendliest, most likeable people I've ever met.' He looked up. There was an unexpected frankness in his stare. 'He's the first... friend I've made since I joined this school.'

'I'm surprised,' said Lucius.

'You shouldn't be. Friendship isn't exactly encouraged around here. We're supposed to feel loyalty to the familia as a whole, but making friends with individual gladiators is... well... I mean, what's the point? We might end up facing each other in the arena.'

'Let's hope you never have to face Trebellius,' said Lucius.

Quin grunted. 'I'd rather not think about that possibility.'

'You all ready for the big day, then?'

'As ready as I'll ever be. You? I can't imagine it's too pleasant down in those tunnels.'

'It's as if Hades* had decided to open a zoo.'

Quin laughed. 'I'm sure you'll get used to it.'

They chatted for a bit longer, then Quin picked up his net and trident and began making his way out of the arena.

'Is Ravilla around?' Lucius called after him, trying to sound casual.

His brother turned and raised an eyebrow. 'He should be. Why?'

Lucius laughed awkwardly. 'Val's got it into her head that she's not seeing enough of her favourite uncle. She wants me to persuade him to invite us both to his house.'

'Good luck with *that*!' snorted Quin. 'I don't think

---

* Hades: the god of the underworld. (The Roman underworld itself was also called Hades.)

I've *ever* been to his house. Have you?'

'Not so far.'

'I rather think he prefers to keep us lot at arm's length. Still – good old Val. I like her spirit! I just hope she's not too hurt when he says no.'

Lucius tried to put Quin's parting comment out of his mind as he made his way up some stairs and down a long corridor towards Ravilla's office in the southeastern corner of the school. He simply *had* to persuade Ravilla to invite them – otherwise the whole plan was doomed!

He knocked and entered the office's antechamber, where Ravilla's secretary worked. The secretary, a Thracian slave named Brasus, with a high, domed forehead and thinning, reddish hair, looked up from a desk piled up with parchments. 'Lucius!' he said severely. 'What are *you* doing here? This is hardly the time for social calls. Ravilla is extremely busy!' Brasus, a sour-faced man of middle years, had never shown the slightest warmth towards his owner's nephew.

'I'll only be a minute,' pleaded Lucius.

'He's with the Prefect of the Vigiles* at the moment, discussing security matters. You'll have to wait.'

Brasus turned back to his papers without even

* *Prefect of the Vigiles: the commander of the city watchmen, who also formed the city fire brigade.*

offering Lucius a seat. Lucius took one anyway and prepared himself for a lengthy wait. He wondered where Isi was, and hoped Silus wasn't expecting them back at the vivarium any time soon.

Perhaps half an hour later, he heard noises from behind the door of Ravilla's office signalling a conclusion to the meeting: chair legs were scraped and voices raised in tones of friendly farewell. A powerful-looking man emerged wearing a purple cloak over leather chest armour and a skirt of white strips with gold trimmings. He strode quickly out of the antechamber without acknowledging either of its occupants.

Ravilla poked his head out of the doorway. 'Brasus, I'm heading out for some lunch shortly. What time is the Governor of Cyprus due?'

'At nona hora,* my lord.'

At that moment, Ravilla noticed Lucius. A brief, slightly anxious look of surprise flickered across his face, then it broadened into an avuncular smile. 'Ah, Lucius! What's happened? Has Silus sacked you for being kind to the animals?'

'Can I speak to you about something, Uncle,' said Lucius. 'I promise it won't take long.'

Ravilla assessed him for a moment, a cool smile playing across his thin, wolfish lips. Then he opened the door wider and gestured for Lucius to enter.

His office was spacious and sunlit, opening onto

* *nona hora: the ninth hour of the day (early afternoon).*

a balcony with a view of the quadrangle below. On his cypress writing table was a silver wine decanter and a pair of goblets engraved with scenes from mythology. Behind the table was an ornate bronze water-clock with a cistern of milky, aquamarine glass. In the corner was a large, painted plaster model of the Flavian Amphitheatre, its four tiers of arcades all carved in exquisite detail. Lucius had to resist a childish urge to touch and explore these expensive and beautiful objects.

'So, what can I do for you?' Ravilla asked him.

He felt his uncle's eyes upon him, trying to see inside his mind. To Ravilla, there was no such thing as an innocent request for a meeting – there was always an ulterior motive to be ferreted out. Lucius, far less practised in the ways of deceit, would now have to tread very carefully. He hoped his amiable smile didn't look forced.

'Uncle, I was talking to Valeria yesterday, and she was lamenting that we never see you these days…'

Ravilla threw his hands up in an exaggerated expression of regret. 'I know, and I'm sorry. Organising these confounded games is taking up every hour of my time. But once they get under way, my workload will greatly diminish, and I promise I shall call on you. Tell me, how *are* dear Caecilia and Valeria?'

'They're both fine, Uncle. But I was wondering if… I mean, it occurred to me that as you're so busy…'

Ravilla waited for him to continue, a puzzled frown

starting to form at Lucius's lengthening pause. 'Yes, what is it?' he prompted.

Now came the decisive moment. Lucius willed himself to speak, aware that his long hesitation was already making him appear suspicious.

'It was Val's idea,' he finally blurted. 'You see, we've never actually been to your house, and…'

Ravilla's frown lifted, and he threw back his head and laughed. 'My little niece wants to pay me a visit? How delightful! But of course. Why don't the three of you come over tomorrow evening? I was expecting the Parthian ambassador, but his wife has fallen ill, so I find myself unexpectedly free, and with a kitchen full of food. I'll send a litter to fetch you at hora prima noctis.'*

'Thank you,' gasped Lucius, his relief submerged beneath a new upswelling of panic: his mother couldn't come! She knew about the letter and was bound to smell a rat! 'I think it may just be me and Val, though,' he added.

'Oh! Why's that?'

'Mother, uh… She gets very tired in the evenings.'

'Understandable, I suppose,' muttered Ravilla. He opened the door. 'Well, until tomorrow then.'

When Lucius returned home from work that evening, he found his mother alone in the apartment, boiling up some mutton and lentil stew on a tiny stove in the kitchen. He was desperate to tell Val the good

* *hora prima noctis: the first hour of the night – around sunset.*

news and he asked his mother where she was.

'You'll find her across the street with that beastly animal – oh yes, she explained her brilliant little scheme to me! I said to her the only trick that creature will ever be good for is destroying fine tableware. But as long as it doesn't come anywhere near me or my property, I don't much care what she does with it.'

As Lucius was dashing out of the apartment his mother called after him: 'Tell her to come in for supper.'

Lucius clattered down the stairs, crossed the street and made his way over to the courtyard where Val had told him she planned to keep Simio. A narrow alleyway led him into a dim, rather depressing space, surrounded on four sides by the backs of tall tenement buildings. Wild oleander bushes sprouted from the cobbles, and ancient vines spilled from cracks in the rough stone walls. In one corner was a series of wooden cages. Squatting on the cobbles next to one of them was Simio. Valeria and her friend Euphemia were seated on a step opposite him, trying to teach him to smile. They made exaggerated grins at the chimp, and each time he copied them they offered him a fig, which he greedily swiped and gobbled down. As Lucius drew closer, he noticed other animals in the cages: a silky-haired Maltese dog with a curly, featherlike tail, a barbary ape and a baboon – both of them young – and a couple of tan-coloured snakes with dark markings, coiled around a branch.

'Simio is *so* clever!' Euphemia informed Lucius

when he reached them. 'We'll have him juggling while riding on a goat's back in no time. He'll be the star of the Forum, you just wait.'

She was a thin, sharp-featured girl, who resembled some sort of animal herself – perhaps a fox or a weasel.

'He's also pretty greedy!' added Val. 'He's nearly cleaned us out of figs.'

'We have to go in for supper,' Lucius told his sister.

'Oh, can't I stay here just a bit longer?' she pleaded.

'We also need to talk!' said Lucius, giving her a meaningful look.

Seeing this, Valeria immediately jumped to her feet. She kissed Simio on the top of his head. 'See you soon, Simmy,' she said, before waving to her friend. 'Same time tomorrow then, Phee!'

'I'll be here.'

As soon as they were back in the street, Valeria turned to Lucius. 'So, what happened? Did he agree?'

Lucius smiled and nodded. 'We've been invited for tomorrow evening. We're to be picked up in a litter at sunset.'

Valeria threw her arms around him in a spontaneous hug of delight. 'See, I told you it'd be easy.'

'But what are we going to tell Mother?'

Valeria frowned a moment, then looked up at him, a mischievous smile dawning on her face. 'Wait here a moment,' she said, before dashing back down the alleyway to the courtyard.

She reappeared five minutes later.

'Where did you go?' he demanded.

Valeria just smiled with impish self-confidence. 'Tomorrow evening, Mother will be out,' she said.

'How do you know?'

'Because Euphemia's father, Gordianus the tailor, will be inviting her over to his apartment for dinner.'

Lucius's shocked look made her giggle.

'How in Hades did you manage to arrange that?'

'Well,' said his sister blithely, 'you know how Gordianus is a widower, and how Mother always blushes whenever I mention his name? It turns out the feeling's mutual. Phee and I have been talking for weeks about getting them together, and this just seems to be the perfect opportunity.'

'But have you forgotten that Mother is married –' Lucius blurted, '– to Father?!'

Val's smile faded a little. 'She doesn't love him, though. If she did, she would have fought to protect his name.'

Lucius had to concede the wisdom of this observation.

'Look, I spend all day with her,' Val continued. 'I know how lonely she is. It would do her good to have some company besides the two of us. Phee's going to speak to her father. She's sure he'll agree to the plan.'

Supper was, as usual, simple and rather bland, and Lucius tried hard to ignore the more flavoursome smells wafting up from Calva's Thermopolium below. As they were tucking in, they heard a soft tread upon the stairs. Val grinned and kicked Lucius under the table. At the first tentative knock, she jumped up to open the door.

Gordianus the tailor stepped shyly across the threshold. He was a small, wiry man, with a kind face and alert eyes. His chin was freshly shaved and Lucius caught a whiff of sweet nardus oil emanating from his greying hair.

Caecilia started when she saw him, and dropped her spoon in her bowl with a splash.

'So sorry to disturb your meal, Caecilia Valeri Aquilae,' said the tailor, 'but I was wondering if you might be free tomorrow evening for uh… for uh…' He faltered.

'Of course!' burst in Val. 'You're free, aren't you, Mother? What time will you be calling on us, sir?'

Gordianus smiled gratefully at the girl. 'At sunset?'

'Could you make it a little earlier,' implored Val. 'Say, duodecima hora?'*

'Valeria!' said Caecilia sharply. She turned, blushing, to Gordianus. 'That is most kind of you, Gnaeus Acilius Gordianus. What is it that you wish me to be free for, exactly?'

Gordianus explained that he wanted to offer her dinner at his apartment. Caecilia graciously agreed.

* *duodecima hora: the twelfth hour of the day – the last hour of daylight.*

A time was arranged for him to call, and he happily departed a few minutes later.

Caecilia glared at Val suspiciously after he'd gone, but said nothing. As Lucius and Val helped clear away the dishes, he spotted his mother picking up a bronze mirror and studying her face in the glass. She was 37. The harshness of her current existence had taken its toll. Her blond hair was not so silky these days, her skin not as creamy-smooth, and her blue eyes had lost something of their lustre, but she was still beautiful. He worried that Val had needlessly complicated their family's plight by setting her up with Gordianus. It solved an immediate problem, but might turn out to have spawned a more serious one further down the road.

Suddenly, they heard thunderous footsteps charging up the stairs. Lucius and Val came out of the kitchen in time to see Quin sweeping into the sitting room. It was a long time since he'd visited, and it seemed to Lucius that his brother had grown altogether too big for their humble apartment. These days he had a presence that could command arenas. His bronzed, muscular figure, which Lucius had observed earlier moving with such fluid dynamism and grace, now seemed cramped and restricted, like that of a caged bear.

In fact, Quin looked devastated. He threw himself into a chair and covered his face with his hands.

'Quin! What's wrong?' cried Caecilia, putting down the mirror.

'Everything!' he groaned.

'Aren't you going to fight in the Inaugural Games?' asked Val.

Lucius's heart lifted at this prospect. He hated it when Quin fought. Perhaps he'd sustained an injury that would keep him out of the games.

Quin opened his eyes and stared dazedly ahead of him. 'Of course I'm going to fight. I'm going to fight Trebellius!' He let out a howl of anguish and bashed a brawny fist against the chair arm.

'Who's Trebellius?' asked Caecilia, but Quin was too enveloped in self-pity to hear her.

'He's Quin's best friend,' explained Lucius.

'I can't do it!' sobbed Quin.

Caecilia spooned some of the remaining stew into a bowl and handed it to him. He took it wordlessly and began to eat, seemingly without tasting a thing. He looked to Lucius at that moment like a man condemned.

'You *have* to fight him,' said Caecilia. 'You took the blood oath, remember? – that means absolute obedience.'

'Of all the Secutores in all the gladiator schools attending the games, why did it have to be him?' Quin groaned.

'When's the fight?' asked Lucius.

'In the afternoon of the opening day – less than three days' time!' He gazed imploringly at Caecilia, as if somehow she held the power to end this torment. 'He's my best friend, Mother.'

'You must do your duty,' said Caecilia coldly. 'You must defeat him.'

'That's as good as killing him!' said Quin. 'It's the opening day. The mob will want to see blood, and the sponsor daren't refuse them.' Quin spat these words out with such venom – as if he suddenly hated the crowd, whose love he'd done so much to court.

'Can't you work something out with your friend?' suggested Val. 'Maybe you could agree to draw.'

Quin looked up at her through his tears. 'Oh, my sweet girl,' he said sadly. 'It's not like a game of latrunculi.* I'm afraid there always has to be a winner in these contests.'

'What will you do?' asked Lucius.

Quin sighed, and a bleak stoicism** entered his expression. 'I have no choice. As Mother says, I signed the oath. Of course I'll have to fight him.'

* latrunculi: a Roman board game.

** stoicism: the belief, very important to the ancient Romans, that one must face up to one's duty or destiny without complaint.

CHAPTER V

3 MARCH

At hora prima noctis the following evening, a litter, shouldered by a crew of six white-liveried bearers from Bithynia in Asia Minor, arrived outside a humble insula in Suburra. Luckily, it was a quiet evening and few were around to witness Lucius and his sister stepping into the litter's velvet-cushioned interior. They were spotted by Calva, though, busy cooking sausages in anticipation of the rush when the taverns closed. The fat proprietor looked most surprised, and not a little envious to see Lucius and Val climbing aboard such a stylish form of transport. Val giggled and gave him a cheeky wave before closing the crimson curtains.

'Be careful,' muttered Lucius as the litter began

its gentle, swaying progress through the streets. 'We don't want him to hate us any more than he already does.'

'Oh, that would be impossible,' she grinned. 'Have you heard the things he says about us to his customers? He calls us offal-eaters, not fit to clean his latrine. Now he knows we're well-connected, he might be more polite.'

'Well, as long as he doesn't say anything to Mother, that's all I care about.'

Soon they had left Suburra behind for a leafier, sweeter-smelling district. They passed a great stone basilica* and a many-pillared temple to Venus. Dominating the horizon to their left was the great edifice of the Flavian Amphitheatre, its travertine marble exterior now suffused with the deep glow of sunset. It was a beautiful sight, yet its rosy sheen made Lucius think of all the blood – human and animal – that would soon be spilt there.

'What's the plan once we leave Ravilla's house?' Val wanted to know.

'Once the litter has brought us home, we're to meet with Isi, hopefully with the red box in her hands, back at Agathon's apartment,' said Lucius. He and Isidora had gone to see Agathon after finishing work earlier that day. Argos had been desperately excited to see him, and had nearly barked the place down. Agathon's

* *basilica: a large public building used for business meetings or as a place to consult lawyers.*

92

approval of the plan had given Lucius an extra boost of confidence – however, he remained all too aware that lots of things could still go wrong.

The litter began to ascend the Palatine Hill.* The road wound upwards, past great mansions with white walls and red roofs, peeping shyly from behind their veils of cypress trees. Eventually they turned in through a guarded, porticoed** entrance. They were set down in an atrium far grander than that of their former home. The walls were covered in delicately painted pastoral scenes. Against the walls, between the frescoes, were placed exquisitely crafted chairs of walnut wood and ivory. The enormous floor mosaic, displaying concentric circles of elaborate wave and knot patterns, had a square pool at its centre to collect rainwater from a hole in the roof directly above. From somewhere in the house came the music of a cithara*** player.

To judge from this room alone, Ravilla was a lot wealthier than Lucius had ever imagined. He knew that his uncle was involved in a whole string of business ventures, not all of them strictly legal, and here was the fruit of all that wheeling and dealing – a luxurious

---

* *Palatine Hill: the most ancient part of Rome, overlooking the Forum Romanum (the main public square) and the Circus Maximus (the stadium for chariot races and other events).*

** *porticoed: decorated with a row of columns.*

*** *cithara: an instrument with seven strings, played with a plectrum – similar to a lyre, but larger and more elaborate.*

mansion in that most exclusive of all Rome's districts, the Palatine Hill.

'It's beautiful here,' breathed Val. 'Why has he never invited us before?'

Lucius wondered about that: was it embarrassment, or simple indifference? But right now he had a more pressing concern than second-guessing Ravilla's motives: how would he ever find his uncle's bedroom? Earlier that day, Isidora had drawn a diagram of the ground-floor layout in the sand of Magnentia's enclosure, and Lucius had done his best to memorise it. He knew the bedroom lay at the top of a marble staircase, but now he couldn't recall where the staircase was in relation to the atrium.

The chief steward entered. He was a swarthy man from Cappadocia in Asia Minor, with a long nose and deeply lined face, who introduced himself as Anastasis. He led them between a pair of slender columns of Phrygian marble and out into the garden. They walked along gravel paths edged with sculpted box hedges. Amid the surrounding acanthus trees and Mediterranean fan palms, they caught glimpses of bronze statues of goatlike satyrs playing panpipes. Pomegranate trees, heavy with lush pink fruit, were reflected in an artificial stream that fed a hexagonal green pool shimmering with golden carp. In the centre of the pool was a bronze dolphin, sculpted in mid-leap, spewing water from its mouth.

'Valeria! Lucius! I bid you welcome!'

They turned to see Ravilla smiling broadly at them from a balustraded terrace. He looked relaxed, beautifully groomed, and watchful, like a sleek forest predator. Ravilla was playing the part of jovial host, yet Lucius detected hints of his uncle's real nature showing through – his mouth continued to smile, but his gaze soon wandered from their faces as he cast a judgemental eye over Lucius's shabby toga praetexta,[*] and the small hole in Val's tunic.

He hates us so much, thought Lucius. *He has destroyed his brother's reputation and made us all wretched with poverty. He has defeated us, yet even now does he feel so insecure that he has to seek these petty proofs of his superiority?*

Lucius and Valeria mounted some steps to the terrace, then followed Ravilla through to the triclinium.[**] More murals filled these walls, this time on themes of food and hunting. Placed in niches between the paintings were beautiful and highly valuable objects: a pair of silver trumpets; a Greek urn; statuettes of Mercury and Apollo in adamantine basalt; and, most impressive of all, a solid gold candelabrum with seven branches. Lucius and Valeria took their places on a pair of couches facing each other across the low table, while their host reclined on the third couch that formed the base of the U.

[*] *toga praetexta: a white toga with a purple stripe, worn by boys, but also by magistrates and other important citizens.*

[**] *triclinium: a formal dining room. The word means 'a place with three couches'; Roman diners did not sit at the table, but reclined on three large couches arranged in a U-shape.*

'You lucky children will enjoy a feast tonight!' boasted Ravilla. 'The kitchen has been well stocked in anticipation of the ambassador's visit, and you are to be the beneficiaries.' There was the slightest sneer in his tone as he said this, and Lucius read a different message into his words: *Eat up, you scroungers – be grateful for this brief taste of the good life before you disappear back to your pathetic rathole in Suburra.*

A servant brought in the first course – an iced platter of oysters – and set it down on the low table. Ravilla explained that they came from the Lucrine Lake in Campania, famed for its oyster beds.

Valeria began gulping them down greedily, until Lucius shot her a warning glance: their stomachs weren't used to this kind of food – the last thing they needed this evening was for her to get sick. That could ruin everything. He was relieved to see her make an effort to slow down.

The oysters were followed by filleted turbot mixed with goose liver and drizzled with a sauce of honey, oil, pounded pepper, lovage and marjoram. Lucius, by now so accustomed to bland and simple fare, was stunned by the exotic smells, textures and tastes.

Then, to his dismay, Valeria made an embarrassing request: 'Uncle, do you have some garum, by any chance?'

Lucius shuddered inwardly. Garum was fermented fish sauce, a condiment used by the poor of Rome to add flavour to their food. Val had unfortunately acquired a taste for it and now liked to put it on everything. This was the ultimate proof, if any were needed, of their decline in status.

Ravilla smirked, as if he had expected nothing else. He summoned a slave and asked him to fetch some Hispanic garum. It arrived in a gilded bowl with a silver spoon. Val daubed it generously on her turbot, and followed this up with sounds of great pleasure as she proceeded to devour everything on her plate.

By the time the roast pheasant arrived, stuffed with herbs and minced quails' eggs, Lucius felt barely able to eat another morsel. Val also looked a little queasy at the prospect of yet another course, having overdone it on the previous two. Ravilla, who had paced himself better, began tucking in. With his uncle thus preoccupied, this would be a good time, Lucius decided, to put their plan into action. The garden beyond the terrace was now shrouded in darkness. Isidora was hopefully already hiding somewhere inside the grounds of the villa.

Lucius caught Val's eye, and she gave an almost imperceptible nod.

'Uncle,' said Lucius, 'do you mind if I use your latrine?'

'Of course, of course!' said Ravilla, waving a greasy pheasant leg in the direction of the doorway. 'Musa!' he called to a slave standing nearby. 'Show Lucius to the latrine, will you?'

'I'm sure I can find my way,' said Lucius.

Ravilla grinned, and picked something from between his teeth. 'I don't want you getting lost, my boy. Musa will show you where it is.'

Lucius slowly got up, a new worry now consuming him – what if he couldn't shake off Musa?

As he made his way out of the room, he heard Valeria embark on her plan of distraction. 'Uncle, please tell me about some of the beautiful objects in this room…'

Musa was a heavily built, bald giant, who, from his fierce look, could easily have found employment as a prison guard or a gladiator. Lucius followed his hulking figure out of the room and along a corridor, past a recess glowing with oil lamps, where the cithara player he'd heard earlier strummed silkily. They passed a statue of Diana the Huntress, a marble staircase guarded by winged Victories, and a room-sized painting of two gladiators in combat – the riches of this house seemed endless.

A marble staircase! That must be the one Isi had mentioned.

Musa directed him through a low, arched entrance to he latrine.

'No need to wait for me,' Lucius tried to assure him. 'I can find my own way back from here.'

'I wait for you,' came the deep-voiced reply. Lucius could only watch in despair as Musa planted himself immovably outside the entrance.

Lucius entered and sat down on the communal lavatory bench. He ran his hands through his hair, trying to think what to do next. How could he shake himself free of the guard's presence? Ravilla's bedroom was at the top of those marble stairs. It would take Lucius no more than twenty seconds to mount the stairs and enter the room, a further twenty to open the window, and twenty more to return to the ground floor – a minute in total. How could he buy himself a minute? He stared at the floor, and then at his sandals. One of the straps was coming loose, and that gave him an idea.

A moment later, Lucius emerged from the toilet.

'I'm ready,' he informed Musa, and the two of them began their return. By the time they reached the marble staircase, the strap on Lucius's left sandal had become quite unravelled. He knelt down and began slowly rewrapping it around his lower leg.

Musa stopped and turned.

'It's all right,' said Lucius. 'I remember the way from here.'

'I wait for you,' said Musa.

'Listen,' pleaded Lucius, pointing around a bend in the corridor. 'I can hear the cithara player. From there, I can easily find my way back.'

'I wait for you,' repeated Musa impassively.

That was when Lucius realised that his uncle must have told the staff to keep a constant watch on him. Did Ravilla suspect something? Of course he did! He was Ravilla!

Despondently, he finished retying his sandal and rose to his feet. They started once more down the corridor. Suddenly, from somewhere near the front of the house, a bell began raucously clanging.

'Nemesis!'* cursed Musa. 'It is alarm! Must be intruder in grounds!'

He raced away in the opposite direction, leaving Lucius churned up with anxiety – it had to be Isi! If she was caught, Ravilla would know for certain that they'd been plotting something tonight, and it wouldn't take him long to figure out what they were after.

Still, there was a remote chance the alarm had nothing to do with Isi – in which case the plan was still on, and he now had the perfect opportunity to fulfill his part of it.

He raced up the marble staircase. At the top was a passageway leading off in both directions. He opened the first door he came to. It turned out to be a library, with a reading couch and wall niches filled with scrolls. The next door along, he was relieved to find, led into the master bedroom. The room had a sweet, drowsy smell, thanks to lamps filled with cinnamon and hyacinth oil that had been placed in the wall niches. A low wooden table, supported by legs shaped like acanthus leaves, held a crystal jug of water and a bowl of fresh figs and dates. Slaves must have been in the room just minutes before, preparing it for their master – Lucius was very lucky to have missed them. The room was dominated by a teak and ivory bed with a gold damask cover, but his eye was immediately drawn to a large cedarwood

* *Nemesis: Musa swears by the goddess of revenge.*

chest at its foot. The red box, according to Isi, had to be in there!

He was sorely tempted to take a look inside the chest, but he knew that he'd run out of time and might be discovered at any second. So he dashed over to the pair of arched windows, unbolted the shutters and then opened them a crack – just enough to allow Isi to use her nails to prise them open from the outside.

He was about to depart the room when he heard footsteps approaching in the passageway outside. It was too late to escape! In a panic, Lucius cast around for a shadowy niche or recess where he could hide. He couldn't find anywhere, and none of the furniture looked big enough to conceal him – except for the bed. He scrambled beneath it just as someone entered the room. Peering through the tassels of the bedcover, Lucius spied a pair of sandalled feet and the hem of a dark red tunic – a house slave. The servant moved towards the middle of the room and stopped. Lucius began to sweat. He'd been careful to keep the shutters almost closed, but if the servant noticed they'd been unbolted, the game would truly be up.

For several long, painful minutes, the slave stood there. Finally, he turned and left the room. Lucius began breathing again. He waited until he was quite sure that the slave was no longer nearby, then he emerged from under the bed, scurried from the room and hurriedly descended the stairs. Luckily, the downstairs corridor was deserted. He took a deep breath, wiped a trickle of sweat from his brow, and returned to the triclinium.

Ravilla and Valeria were standing by one of the wall niches. Ravilla was showing Val the solid gold candelabrum. They both looked up when Lucius entered.

'Lucius!' cried Ravilla. 'You missed all the excitement. There's been some commotion or other outside. I think we may have had an intruder...'

He paused and studied Lucius with eyes suddenly narrowed with suspicion. Lucius's heart thumped in his chest like the hammer of Vulcan, the blacksmith god. He felt Ravilla's piercing stare like a red-hot poker, burning its way through to the truth.

Then, to his great relief, Ravilla's face lightened. 'Don't worry,' he said carelessly, 'the guards are dealing with it. Come over here. Your sister was asking me about this.'

Was Ravilla playing games with them – had he worked out their real motives in coming here? And what about Isi? If she was caught and dragged into this room, there would be no longer any point in pretending innocence. With these fears eating away at him, Lucius obligingly looked at the candelabrum. It had a central stem, out of which curved six branches – three on each side.

'It's so beautiful,' said Val, peering at the delicate scrollwork on its base.

'It's a personal gift from the emperor,' said Ravilla proudly. 'It comes from the Jewish temple in Jerusalem, which he destroyed during the siege exactly ten years ago. It's called a Menorah – one of their most sacred relics, apparently.'

Anastasis entered, closely followed by Musa. The chief steward bowed. 'My Lord, I apologise for the disturbance just now.'

'What was its cause?' asked Ravilla.

Lucius dug his nails deep into his palms to stop himself from shaking. He noticed that his sister's face had gone as white as chalk powder. Her eyes remained fixed on the candelabrum.

'A fortune-teller came to the door, my Lord,' reported Anastasis. 'While the door was open, the man's dog escaped into the atrium. I'm afraid the porter panicked and raised the alarm. Both fortune-teller and dog have now been removed from the property, and the porter has been reprimanded for his carelessness and over-reaction. I hope the incident did not spoil your evening.'

Lucius sighed inwardly – so the intruder wasn't Isi! Then his body gave an involutary shiver. *A dog?*

The remainder of the evening passed much too slowly for Lucius. All he wanted was to get back to Agathon's and find out what had happened. Instead, he had to feign enthusiasm for the beautifully arranged platter of figs, nuts, grapes and plums that was brought to the table, and pretend interest in Ravilla's gloating stories about his many meetings with the emperor and senior members of the imperial court.

At last, with Valeria stifling yawns, Ravilla rose

from his couch and wished them good night. Anastasis escorted them to the entrance, where their litter was waiting for them. Half an hour later they were back outside their insula in Suburra. They waited for the litter bearers to depart before setting off at a fast jog along the side streets and alleyways towards the Velabrum.

Argos greeted them with loud, excited barks at the door of Agathon's apartment. 'Come in! Come in!' cried Agathon. 'Oh, what an adventure we've had tonight.'

Isidora was seated cross-legged on the floor, a triumphant grin on her face. Lucius and Valeria could only stare in open-mouthed wonder at the object on the floor in front of her. It was a plain box of scuffed red leather, with a tarnished bronze lock.

'You got it!' they chorused.

'Of course I did,' said Isi nonchalantly. 'Did you ever doubt me?'

Lucius fell to his knees and grasped the box reverently as if it contained the legendary prophecy, the Oracles of the Sibyl. 'Have you opened it yet?' he asked.

'I insisted we wait for you two,' said Agathon. 'You are Aquila's kin. It's only right that you should be here for this moment.'

Lucius noticed that Agathon was wearing a tunic

marked with strange, mystic symbols. He spotted a horoscope chart in the corner, and his suspicions about the role his former tutor had played this evening were confirmed. 'You were the fortune-teller!' Lucius cried. 'And you!' he added, hugging Argos, 'were the fortune-teller's dog, you wicked animal!'

'Why did you do it, Agathon?' asked Valeria, her eyes sparkling with curiosity.

'We needed to provide a distraction for the guards so that Isidora could break in,' Agathon explained. He looked apologetically towards Lucius. 'We didn't tell you because we feared you wouldn't approve of using Argos in that way. But I can assure you, he played his part brilliantly.'

'And so did you, Lucius!' said Isi admiringly. 'I was outside Ravilla's bedroom window when that servant came in and you had to scramble under the bed. My heart was in my mouth, I can tell you!'

'I think we should all be very proud of ourselves tonight,' Lucius sighed contentedly, 'including Val, who kept Ravilla talking about his precious objects while the theft was taking place. But now we must see if all our efforts have been worth anything.' He looked down at the box nestling in his hands. 'I can only pray that my father is right and the letter that will save him is in here.'

Agathon took the box from Lucius and began working the tip of his knife under its lid. Ten very tense minutes later, the lid finally snapped open. They all stared at the interior of the box. It contained a pair of clay dice, a wooden model of a horse, the skull of a bird of prey, a metal brooch, a tin bugle and a dagger in a leather sheath.

There was no letter.

PART TWO

THE GAMES

CHAPTER VI

5 MARCH

The city had not witnessed such excitement since Emperor Titus's triumphal procession ten years earlier. Today was the opening day of the long-awaited Inaugural Games of the Flavian Amphitheatre. The citizens of Rome had watched in awe and anticipation as the amphitheatre – Vespasian's 'Palace of the People' – had gone up, tier upon gleaming tier. Now, for the first time, they would be allowed to enter its portals and see with their own eyes its pristine oval of glittering white sand. For weeks the city's notice writers had been publicising the games, attracting eager throngs wherever they set up their ladders. Their painted postings promised a show that would last more than a hundred days, featuring exotic animals from distant realms, prisoner executions, battle recreations and mouth-watering contests between champion gladiators from all the top schools of Italia. Every mention of the current favourite, Quintus Felix, was guaranteed to raise a hearty cheer among the watching crowds.

As the big day dawned, drums could be heard across the city, pounding out an urgent rhythm. The streets were soon swarming with people of every walk of life, from perfumed nobles to Suburran thugs, all of them converging on the amphitheatre. Among this throng were Lucius and Isidora. Lucius's mouth was as dry as a bone. To him, the drumbeats felt like a death march. The amphitheatre, looming ever closer, was a ravenous monster, its rows of pillars and arches like bared teeth. Burnished shields set in the arches of the topmost tier blazed in the rising sun like a row of evil, glinting eyes.

Isidora, noting his desolate, fearful look, took his hand. 'We'll keep the animals calm,' she reassured him. 'Their final hour in our care will be as happy as we can make it.'

Lucius tried to smile, appreciating her attempt to comfort him, but his sorrow was too deep for simple words to soothe. Along with all the animals now imprisoned in their cages, he felt, with every step, his own impending death. For what was the point of living in a world of such bitter injustice, where the wicked thrived and the innocent suffered? The games were being paid for by the emperor, but they were a triumph for Ravilla, the chief organiser, as much as for Titus. And Ravilla, Lucius now feared, was untouchable – his power and prestige had grown too immense. The letter from the previous emperor, Vespasian – their one hope of exposing Ravilla's dark secret to the world – would probably never be discovered.

'Do you suppose my father was wrong about the letter?' he asked Isidora. 'Do you think he was misinformed? Maybe it doesn't even exist.'

Isidora looked at him, surprised. 'You're not thinking about *that* today? I thought you were concerned for the animals.'

'I am, but… for me, it's all connected. While my father remains in exile – while the man who destroyed him grows more powerful – I feel as caged as any of those animals. And if there is to be no hope of justice in the end, then I may just as well enter the arena with the lions and hyenas and be speared by a Bestiarius.'

After a pause, Isidora said: 'Don't despair, Lucius. I'm sure the letter exists, but maybe Ravilla guessed we were going to try and steal it, and removed it from the red box. It's somewhere in his house. We just have to try again. And we will.'

A wooden barricade had been set up in front of the lowest tier of the amphitheatre to control the crowd. Next to this were vendors renting out cushions, or selling sausages, pastries, boiled eggs and spiced wine. Even at this early hour, long queues had already formed before the marble entrances located at every fourth arch of the amphitheatre.

Lucius and Isidora approached a guard and showed him their passes – flat pieces of bone inscribed with the name of their vivarium. He let them through the barricade and they descended once more into the hellish labyrinth of subterranean tunnels known as the Hypogeum. The smell of torch smoke was combined with the sweet stench of animal fear, and the noise of caged beasts crashing against their constraints – the guttural roars of lions, the screams of leopards and the mad laughter of hyenas – echoed through the stone corridors.

Silus had yet to arrive, so Lucius and Isidora got straight on with their rounds, checking on the animals in their charge. Lucius found Magnentia huddled in a corner of her cage, unnerved by the screeching and yowling of her fellow captives, the flickering torchlight and the incessant beating of the drum. The statue of Titus, which he'd painstakingly glued back together, stood in the opposite corner. Lucius had told Silus that he'd finally coaxed her to kneel before the statue – he hadn't, but he was scared Silus would kill her if he knew the truth.

Lucius tempted Magnentia out of her corner with a bucket of fruit and tender young plants. While she ate her breakfast, he applied more resin and cream to the wound she'd received from Silus. All the while, he murmured soothing words to her. She would have to fight today. Lucius had no doubt she would win – she had killed every elephant or bull set against her. What concerned him was what would happen after that. As the victor, she was expected to kneel before the emperor. This was the tradition in elephant combats, going back to the time of the first emperor, Augustus. Lucius's one remaining hope was that, even though Magnentia had spurned the emperor's image, she would do her duty when faced with the majesty of the man himself.

Once all his animals were fed and watered, Lucius ascended to the upper tier of tunnels. Heading down a corridor, he passed by pens containing antelopes, stags and boars, until he reached one of the caged entrances set into the perimeter wall. The pure white sand of the arena, specially shipped in from North African beaches, sparkled like a lake of diamonds before him.

Above the black marble perimeter wall, which was more than three times the height of a man, tier upon tier of seating seemed to reach almost to the sky. Above the topmost tier was a wooden platform on which could be seen the tiny figures of hundreds of sailors, drafted in from the naval ports of Ostia and Misenum. To the rhythm of the drum, the sailors were heaving on ropes, raising the velarium – the vast, colourful sailcloth awning that would shelter the spectators during the hottest part of the day. As the great canvas sheet slowly unfurled, it cast deep, glowing shadows across the amphitheatre, tinting the marble terraces with shifting shades of red, yellow, turquoise and green. But the velarium only extended over the audience, leaving the arena itself exposed – those who were to fight and die here would do so in the full glare of the sun.

As Lucius watched, officials called locarii began guiding the spectators to their seats. First to be allowed in were the senators, with their purple-bordered togas, who occupied the first eighteen rows. Equites, the lower class of nobles, took up the rows immediately behind. A flourish of trumpets announced the arrival of the emperor. Lucius turned to look at the imperial box, positioned on a raised podium on the long northern curve of the arena. The box was flanked by laurel-entwined columns surmounted by gold eagles. Its silk curtains were thrown open – Lucius had heard that Titus never liked to hide himself from public view. By squinting, Lucius could just make out the emperor's purple-robed figure amid the silver and crimson of his elite bodyguards, the Praetorian Guard. Other important people flowed into the amphitheatre: magistrates, noblemen, visiting dignitaries, and Rome's most sacred priestesses, the Vestal Virgins.

When all the nobility were seated, the plebeians – the ordinary citizens of Rome – were allowed in. They arrived in a rush, a great torrent of elbowing, jostling humanity, fanning out across the upper tiers – merchants and wealthy plebeians in front, poorer citizens behind. Following them in was a stampede of freedmen, plebeian women and slaves disguised as citizens, who occupied the wooden gallery seating at the very highest level.

The babble of the crowd gradually hushed as slaves began erecting an altar to Jupiter Latiaris[*] in the centre of the arena. The chief priest and his attendants, dressed in white robes with red scarves, gathered there for the sacrifice. From an entrance on the opposite side to where Lucius stood, a white bull was led out by attendants. The bull, pampered and indulged throughout its life, seemed perfectly content. It did not expect the blade of the axe as it smashed down on its neck. Death was sudden and immediate. Lucius sensed a flinching movement to his right. He turned to see Isi standing beside him, her eyes wide and damp. They watched together in silence as the chief priest cut into the bull's belly, examined its entrails and declared that the gods were favourable to the games.

'Silus has arrived,' whispered Isi. 'Straight after the inaugural procession, we must go below.'

Over the past few days, Lucius and Isidora had endured exhaustive rehearsals of the parts they would have to play today. They knew which organ, horn and drum signals to listen out for, and what each of these meant. They knew where their animals were, and which tunnel or elevator shaft they would need to herd them into when the time came. Like a pair of tiny cogs

[*] *Jupiter Latiaris: the title given to the god Jupiter in his role as defender of the Romans and their earliest allies.*

117

in a giant, well-oiled machine, they wouldn't need to think, only act – and that was probably a good thing.

The inaugural procession entered the arena through the Gate of Life. A cohort of the Praetorian Guard led the way. Weapons and armour gleaming, they marched to the sound of horns, flutes, drums and a water organ. Behind them came floats pulled by teams of zebras with glittering harnesses, upon which stood towering effigies of gods and goddesses.

Next, accompanied by excited screams from the crowd, came the gladiators. Rank after rank of them trooped in – plume-helmeted Samnites, fish-helmeted Secutores, Retiarii with their nets and tridents, and Postulati armed with swords and maces. Lucius strained his eyes, but could not pick out Quin in the dense mass of fighters.

The trainers followed – scarred survivors of the arena – and, after them, representatives of the empire's military talent: Parthian archers, Sarmatian cavalry, Thracian light infantry, Greek hoplites and German swordsmen. Elephants arrived bearing howdahs on their backs, bristling with Nubian spearmen. Then came beast fighters: some leading leopards on chains, others draped with serpents or driving chariots drawn by ostriches. Weaving their way through these fighters were boys dressed as cupids, with gold-dusted hair and skin. With their toy bows, they shot little arrows into the crowd with money prizes attached. Dancing girls with tambourines appeared with garlands of flowers in their hair, and dwarfs tumbled around them doing somersaults and cartwheels.

The procession slowly looped its way around and then out of the arena. Last to leave were the gladiators, milking the cheers as they waved to their supporters in the crowd.

'Time to go!' said Isidora.

They set off at a trot down the corridor, almost colliding with animal handlers coming the other way, heading for the upper-tier cells. They ran down stone steps into the bowels of the Hypogeum, beneath the arena itself. The heat and the chaos hit them like a shockwave. Beastmasters were yelling commands as animal handlers and slaves rushed around. Huge animals, driven to a frenzy of fear and excitement, bucked and kicked and roared. Hinges whined as giant gates swung open. Handlers used whips and firebrands to drive the rhinos, bulls, leopards, bears and hyenas from their cages, up tunnels and into waiting elevators. Heavily muscled Bestiarii huddled in groups, rinsing their mouths with posca, the traditional mixture of vinegar and water that they always drank before the hunt.

When Lucius and Isidora reached Silus, he looked on the verge of bursting a blood vessel. His face was purple, his eyes popping with rage. 'Where've you two been? This isn't a holiday! Get to your stations – NOW!'

They ran to the cage where their bulls were stamping

their hooves and butting the iron bars in panic. With shouts and prods, but no firebrands, the two of them managed to coax four of the animals into the corridor and herded each of them, just in time, into a separate elevator.

A horn blasted, and all around the Hypogeum came the echo of elevator doors slamming shut. Teams of slaves went to work pushing at the arms of the capstans – the great cross-shaped winches that raised the elevators into position just below the arena floor. The capstans creaked as the slaves pushed and trudged slowly in circles. It took eight men – two on each arm of the capstan – to raise one large animal.

Another horn blast signalled that all the animals were in position, either in the elevator shafts below the arena or at the perimeter gates. From above came a steady pounding of the drums, and then a breathless hush stole through the amphitheatre. The Master of the Games, in his box beside the imperial podium, gave the signal, relayed by spotters to the handlers below. Catches were released, bolts were thrown, and suddenly hundreds of animals began pouring into the arena – erupting like magic out of the 36 trapdoors hidden beneath the sand, or bursting from the gates in the perimeter wall. They fanned out across the sand in every direction: bulls, jackals, stags, boars, bears, lions, rhinos, goats, cheetahs, wolves, antelopes, donkeys and hyenas.

All Lucius could hear at first was the deafening

clatter of hooves and paws above his head. Then, above this, like a piercing note on a water organ, came the excited screaming of the spectators, blending with roars and frightened grunts from the arena. He imagined the meat-eaters leaping on the backs of the grazing animals, dragging them to the ground in clouds of sand and blood, and he was relieved that he didn't have to witness the slaughter. Soon, he knew, Parthian archers would appear high up on the perimeter wall, and fire arrows into the mass of beasts, killing scores of them. In the tunnels nearby, assistants were arming the Bestiarii with swords, shields, spears and pikes, ready for the venatio – the wild-beast hunt. They would shortly be heading up into the mêlée, to add to the carnage.

'Lucius! Scenery!' yelled Silus. He realised then that he'd been staring transfixed at the creaking roof of the Hypogeum. He tried to blink away the bloodstained images in his head, then ran to help the other workers load plaster models of green hillocks, trees and bushes into the elevators. The arena was to be transformed into a pastoral scene of forests, groves and clearings in time for the venatio, to give the impression of a real-life hunt. From other elevators, he could hear the whine of the packs of dogs that would be released to assist the Bestiarii.

The hour that followed was a blur of feverish activity, moving scenery and herding increasingly frantic animals into the elevators. They were driven wild by the smell of blood, which now floated thickly on the air. As he worked, Lucius glimpsed freshly slaughtered beasts being dragged on hooks along corridors. The moans of the crowd swelled to a crescendo above his head and it seemed to him that he was feeding a ravening beast that would never be satisfied, however much flesh and blood he gave it.

At last, the crowd quietened. The venatio was over. Stretchers bore wounded Bestiarii to the sickrooms, while the dead and dying animals were hauled through the Gate of Death to the spoliarium – the room where they would be butchered, so their flesh could be sold to the masses or used to feed the carnivores.

While the arena was being cleared of scenery and the bloody sand raked over, Lucius went to see Magnentia. It was her turn now. She'd retreated to her corner again, intimidated by all the noise and the stench of death.

'Come on, girl,' he murmured softly. 'Time to go.' He led her gently out of her cage and down the aisle to the waiting elevator.

Isidora was coming the other way, carrying a bucket of steaming water and a roll of cotton swabs. 'Good luck,' she said. 'I mean to you *and* Magnentia – this is a big moment for both of you!'

'Thanks,' said Lucius. 'How's Kato?'

'He's doing well. Still building up his strength. He won't be fighting for a few more weeks, thankfully.'

'Where are you off to?'

'Lending a hand to the animal surgeons,' she called over her shoulder. 'Some of the lightly wounded ones may live to fight again – poor brutes! But I'll see if I can grab a moment to watch you!'

A flourish of trumpets from above announced the start of a new phase of the show. Silus arrived, and he and Lucius joined Magnentia in the elevator. The beastmaster was relaxed and beaming. 'That went well, didn't it, lad? You heard the crowd just now – they lapped it up! The emperor has to be pleased.'

The slaves began cranking the capstan and, with a reluctant grind and creak, the elevator began to rise. The trapdoor opened in the middle of the arena, and Lucius blinked in the bright sunshine. Magnentia, accustomed to darkness after days spent underground, started backwards in surprise.

Silus leapt up the wooden steps and onto the sand. Seeing the elephant hesitate, he snarled and cracked his whip. 'Get on out there! NOW!'

Magnentia didn't move. Lucius prodded her gently with his ankus. 'Come on, girl,' he coaxed. He saw her big eye blinking slowly. She made a snuffling sound and brushed his cheek with her trunk in a gesture of trust. Then she climbed the steps into the arena. The crowd gasped and applauded her immense size and the impressive length of her curving yellow tusks. The other elephant appeared soon afterwards, along with its trainer, from a different trapdoor, eliciting even louder cheers. Lucius saw at once that he was a bull elephant – bigger than Magnentia, and more massive than any creature she'd yet fought. Luckily, she didn't seem intimidated. As the bull approached her, she trumpeted her war cry and trotted a few paces towards him.

The other trainer was goading his beast with a sharply pointed ankus, infuriating him with a series of little jabs to his hindquarters. The elephant flapped his ears like great flags. He pawed the ground and blew sand clouds through his trunk. Then he gave a great bellow and charged. Magnentia stubbornly stood her ground. As they collided, Lucius heard a loud hollow clunk of tusk on tusk. Their raised trunks twirled and knotted like angry snakes. The bull elephant used his greater size and weight to force Magnentia backwards. He pushed his trunk over her head, grazing her ears with his tusks.

'What's wrong with her?' Silus growled to Lucius. 'She's useless. If she loses this I'm holding you personally responsible.'

'She's never fought an elephant this size before,' said Lucius defensively. 'She's doing her best.' He watched despairingly as Magnentia continued to be forced backwards.

'Her best isn't good enough,' spat Silus. 'She'd better pray she dies now, because I'm going to roast her slowly on a spit for this pathetic display.'

Unable to restrain himself any longer, Silus ran towards the retreating animal and unleashed his whip at her, stinging her back. Magnentia roared with surprise and pain and jerked her head around. The bull elephant took advantage and sank a tusk into her neck.

Lucius cried out as if the dark blood he saw streaming from her was his own. Magnentia went wild. She rose onto her hind legs and delivered a raucous, brassy scream to the skies. Silus scrambled hurriedly backwards as she rampaged towards him, with the bull elephant in hot pursuit. Then, just as it seemed that she would trample him, she swerved. The bull elephant continued lumbering forwards.

'Help!' screamed Silus, now certain he would be killed.

Lucius hurtled forward and pushed Silus to the ground, out of the path of the bull elephant – and because of this, and all the dust swirling around, he missed what happened next. Magnentia wheeled around and struck, quite suddenly, stabbing the bull elephant low down on his unprotected flank.

The giant beast sank to his knees, his eyes clouded with pain. From the amount of blood pouring from his belly, it was clear to all that the wound was mortal. His groans and bellows echoed around the amphitheatre. There were scattered cheers, but the response of most of those watching was respectful silence at the downfall of this noble creature. For once, Lucius was grateful to the Parthian archers, who unleashed their plumed darts to cut short the elephant's suffering.

Lucius struggled to calm Magnentia, who was still shaking her head and trumpeting her outrage. 'Don't fret, my girl,' he said as he leaned his cheek against her and spread his hands across her hot skin, 'I'll take care of you.' The wound in her neck looked bad, but not life-threatening. If she would only do her duty now and kneel before the emperor, Silus might let her live, and Lucius could take care of her. Everything depended on how she performed in the next few minutes.

Just as Lucius felt her grow calmer, an incensed, dust-covered Silus clambered back to his feet. His knees were bloodied, his lips foam-flecked and scowling. 'She-devil!' he bawled. 'Gorgon! How dare she!'

On seeing him approach, Magnentia bellowed again and a violent shudder coursed through her body. Her eyes turned blood-red and Lucius feared that she would gore the beastmaster. He hastily grabbed Silus by the shoulders and pulled him away from her. 'You have to be calm now. If you want her to… to perform for the emperor, you must stop frightening her!'

Lucius had never manhandled Silus before, nor spoken to him in this way. The beastmaster's shoulder muscles flexed. His face turned livid and he looked ready to break Lucius in his brawny fists. But he managed to suppress his fury. 'I will talk to you about this later,' he whispered through savagely gritted teeth. Then he turned towards the imperial box and his face reconfigured itself into an obsequious smile.

'Ave, Caesar!'* he cried, raising his right arm in salute. 'May I present to you… the victor!'

There was a chorus of trumpets, and the water organ began a lurching, wailing melody as Silus, Magnentia and Lucius proceeded towards Titus's podium. Silus led the way, and tried his best to make it appear that he was the one in control of the elephant – but it was clear to all in the stadium that the creature wanted nothing to do with him and was only following him because of discreet prods from Lucius.

When they reached the imperial box, Lucius couldn't resist glancing upwards. The emperor was there, leaning forward in his seat, an indulgent smile at play on his plump, square-jawed face. Among the favoured guests seated alongside him was Ravilla, grinning down on Lucius like a hyena who has just stolen a lion's dinner.

Seeing that triumphant smirk, Lucius was suddenly sure that Ravilla knew what their true purpose had been the other evening at his house. He'd been playing with them all along. If only the emperor, now seated to Ravilla's left, could be told the truth. He was the one man who could rectify everything, and there he was sitting just a few paces away. But Lucius was only too aware that he and the emperor were, in fact, worlds apart. He'd have to fight through countless layers of advisors, courtiers, officials and guards to reach that pleasant-looking, smiling man.

* *Ave, Caesar!: Hail, Emperor!*

127

Silus was gesturing to Lucius impatiently. 'Get on with it!' he hissed.

Lucius gulped. This was the moment. At least Magnentia seemed calmer now. He leaned forwards and slowly slid the tip of the ankus down the back of her front leg – the prompt to kneel. Then he waited.

Magnentia didn't move.

Lucius tried it once more.

Still she remained standing.

'Come on, my girl,' he pleaded into her ear. 'There'll be three buckets of the sweetest, juiciest grass if you'll only kneel for me now.'

She flapped her ears and snorted, but continued to stand in the presence of the most powerful man in the known world.

Silus's expectant grin froze on his face, then crumpled into an embarrassed gape as he sensed impending humiliation. Desperately, he pulled on Magnentia's trunk, but she casually brushed him off, making him stagger sideways and almost lose his footing for the second time that morning.

As the crowd laughed uproariously, Silus turned on Lucius. 'What's going on?' he demanded. 'You promised me…' Then, realising that something was now expected of him, he turned with a servile grin to Titus.

'Caesar, I most humbly apologise for this… this monstrous insubordination. I swear to you that I will have this traitorous beast slaughtered this very afternoon and have her flesh made into cutlets for your hounds.'

Titus fell into a frown on hearing this. 'You shall do no such thing,' he murmured, supporting his chin on his pudgy, ringed hand. Then he rose slowly to his feet, lifted his head and addressed the crowd.

'Ten years ago,' he cried, his rich, commanding voice ringing out around the now-silent amphitheatre, 'I celebrated a triumph through this city's streets. Some of you may remember it! In my carriage there was a slave holding a golden wreath above my head. As I waved to the throngs gathered along the route, the slave whispered into my ear: *Respice post te, hominem te memento* – Look behind you, remember you are only a man. *Memento mori* – Remember that you are mortal... Over the years since then, I have, from time to time, had cause to forget those wise words. It's difficult, when everyone I meet these days treats me like a god!' This remark elicited much sycophantic laughter from the senatorial seats. 'But this brave and stubborn beast has reminded me once again of those words. It is good that the elephant did not bow down before me, as all humans unthinkingly do. For this salutary reminder of my humanity, I am deeply thankful. And I would like to show my gratitude by offering life to this creature, and a place in the gardens of my palace, to live out the remainder of its days in peace, health and tranquillity.' The emperor sat down to thunderous applause and hurrahs from the crowd.

Lucius was stunned at first. Then, as Titus's words sank in, a wonderfully warm feeling began to creep through his insides. Not only would Magnentia live, she would live happily – and there was nothing Silus could do about it. He watched the frown compete with the smile on the beastmaster's bewildered face. Silus was struggling to understand what had just happened. Was the emperor *rewarding* this defiance of his authority? Was he showing *compassion* to this treacherous creature? The beastmaster's lips twitched, his shoulders slumped, and he forced his body into a bow.

'Very good, great Caesar!' he croaked. 'Very wise.'

CHAPTER VII

5–6 MARCH

n the afternoon, the gladiators fought. The opening event was a dramatic battle re-enactment involving hundreds of novices from Ravilla's school, the Ludus Romanus, and their peers from the rival Ludus Claudia. Together they recreated the Roman general Agricola's famous conquest of the Ordovices, a tribe of western Britannia, four years earlier.

For this show, the amphitheatre's architect-engineers had designed a timber fortress to represent the Ordovices' stronghold, with walls twice the height of a man. Lucius and Isidora were among the scores of carpenters' assistants responsible for assembling the replica at top speed in the centre of the arena. It was gruelling work that left Lucius with splintered hands and an aching back, but at least he got to spend some time above ground.

While he was busy with his hammer and nails, Lucius caught sight of a contingent of white-liveried imperial servants heading down into the Hypogeum. He guessed what their purpose was and raced after them, reaching them as they entered the animal injuries room. Magnentia stood there, towering above the other animals, the gash in her neck freshly dressed. Lucius broke through the ranks of palace servants and approached her. He reached up and stroked her cheek, just in front of her ear. She gave a little snort and placed her trunk on his shoulder. She laid it so gently there, it felt as soft as a baby.

'Goodbye, old girl,' he whispered, looking into her slow-blinking eye. 'You're off to a new life now. You'll be looked after – better than I can.'

With tears in his eyes, he turned to one of the servants. 'Her name is Magnentia,' he said. 'She loves green grass, and peaches, and the roots of young plants.'

Then he ran quickly from the room.

The assault on the fortress began just after nona hora, and the result was, of course, a stunning victory for the Romans. The novices on both sides fought bravely, if none too skilfully, and at least half of them fell to an enemy sword. The slaughter, sickening to Lucius, drew rapturous cheers from the terraces. He was dumbfounded by the crowd's delight – the same crowd who just a few hours earlier had been moved to tears by the emperor's compassionate treatment of an elephant.

When the Ordovician fort had been dismantled, the corpses removed and the bloody sand raked over, it was time for the single combat. After another blast on the horns, the Master of the Games made the announcement everyone had been waiting for: 'Retiarius Quintus Felix, the so-called Phoenix of Pompeii, is to fight a recent arrival in our city, former champion of the School of Calabria, Secutor Julianus Trebellius!' These words brought the biggest cheers of the day.

Lucius raced to finish his work so that he could get upstairs in time to see the fight. He found his way to a room beneath the stands, with a row of iron-barred viewing windows just above the level of the arena. Jostling to find a decent position among the many off-duty slaves gathered there, he was in time to see the two gladiators, with their entourage, enter through the Gate of Life. A pair of Numidian boys entered first, bearing Quin's net and trident and Trebellius's sword on crimson silk cushions. Behind them came four more red-liveried servants bearing their armour. Finally, Quin and Trebellius themselves emerged into the sunlight. Unusually, they walked hand in hand in a spirit of friendly comradeship.

If this breach of etiquette caused mutterings of disquiet among the senatorial class, it was drowned out by the great noise that erupted from the poorer seats above them. For, at the first sight of Quin, the upper tiers of the amphitheatre exploded with ecstatic whoops and cheers. It was the bursting of a dam of expectation that had been building steadily for many weeks. He was the one they had paid to come and see. Some, who really did believe he'd risen from the dead, lost all self-control on seeing him, and raced from their seats in a vain attempt to reach the arena, hoping for a touch of his immortal flesh. But they were stopped by guards before they could reach the perimeter wall.

The trumpets sounded, and the stadium gradually quietened. The bearers removed the gladiators' cloaks and presented them with their weapons and armour. For a Retiarius like Quin, success depended on speed and agility, so he fought without a helmet, shield or leg guard. His only defences were the manica and galerus – the arm guard and shoulder guard– and his weapons were the three-pronged trident, a circular net of hemp rope fastened to his wrist, and a straight-bladed dagger called a pugio.

The advantages of the Secutor, by contrast, lay in his greater size, weight and physical strength. Trebellius wore a smooth, round, close-fitting helmet with two small eye-holes. He was further protected by a leather manica on his right arm and wrist, a metal greave on his lower left leg, and a large rectangular shield. His only weapon was a sword.

Their duties done, the attendants retired from the arena. Only the combatants remained, along with four under-trainers, standing in the shadow of the imperial box, equipped with whips and firebrands to goad reluctant fighters. Their presence might have been necessary for novices and prisoners of war who were forced to fight here, but was a mere formality in such a bout as this, between veteran fighters.

The trumpets delivered a second, piercing blast, and the fight commenced. The mid-afternoon sun shimmered on the sand like white fire. It gleamed on their oiled skin as Quin and Trebellius circled each other in the middle of the arena. Trebellius struck first, bringing his sword down like a hammer towards Quin's unprotected head. Quin shifted his upper body with the flexibility of a serpent, evading the strike and at the same time stabbing with his trident. Trebellius parried this with his shield and struck again with his sword, sweeping it around in a semicircle that passed within a fly's wing of Quin's stomach. Quin whirled around and thrust upwards towards his opponent's eye-holes, but Trebellius dodged and counterstruck towards Quin's back. Quin writhed to evade this, then dispatched his net towards Trebellius's head. Trebellius darted to one side and the net fell harmlessly from his helmet. Quin twirled his trident one-handed, transforming it into a downward-stabbing fork, but before he could impale Trebellius's undefended thigh, his adversary nimbly flitted beyond reach.

All these moves and countermoves took place at dizzying speed over a period of seconds, and it took a practised eye to see exactly what was happening. This was a virtuoso display of fighting skill between two men who were masters of their craft but also intimately acquainted with each other's styles. The crowd watched in awe as the pair continued to run through their seemingly endless repertoire of parries, thrusts, twirls, blocks and reverse strikes. It reminded Lucius of the practise fight he'd witnessed at the school, when they had seemed like partners in a bizarre and deadly dance. Their concentration must be intense, their stamina phenomenal, for not once in the long minutes of this battle did the pace let up or the movements slow. And there was nothing half-hearted about their efforts – every one of their blows, if it had landed, looked to be fatal. And yet, as the performance continued, a restlessness began to steal over the crowd. They weren't used to seeing such a well-matched pair. They wanted blood.

A chant began high up in the wooden galleries, quickly spreading from the freedmen to the poor plebeians and from there to the wealthy merchants and traders:

Quintus! Quintus! Quintus Felix! Iugula! Verbera! Ure!
'Slit his throat! Beat him! Burn him!'

Suddenly, as if at some secret signal only they could hear, the two men stopped fighting. For a moment, they simply stared at each other, as motionless as a pair of training dummies. The entire amphitheatre fell into a stunned silence at this unaccountable behaviour. All that could be heard was the ghostly creaking of the velarium ropes high above.

Did they plan this? Lucius wondered. *What are they going to do now?*

Eventually, Trebellius and Quin both turned to the imperial box. Trebellius took off his helmet and they let their weapons fall with a clatter to the ground. Then they clasped hands and raised them high above their heads.

The shocked silence was ruptured by a cacophony of outraged cries, yells, boos and catcalls. It was unheard of for gladiators to break off a fight, let alone make such an unseemly display of friendship. What was the world coming to? They were supposed to fight to the death! They had sworn an oath!

Hesitantly at first, the under-trainers advanced towards the centre of the arena. Then, goaded by the crowd, they marched more purposefully up to the rebel pair.

'Fight!' yelled one of them, and he cracked his whip, raising a cloud of dust.

The two gladiators remained where they were, blinking in the stirred-up sand, their clasped hands still raised high.

'Fight!' screamed another under-trainer, and he thrust a red-hot iron at Trebellius's chest.

Trebellius screamed. He broke away from Quin and staggered backwards.

A third under-trainer raised his weighted whip. The seven-thonged scourge was fitted with steel balls to inflict extra pain. He lashed Quin's back. The Retiarius flinched, but didn't cry out. The under-trainer thrashed him again and again – thirteen times in all. Everyone observed how his skin was lacerated into a map of angry red lines – and how he never made a sound. Then the second under-trainer moved in close. Everyone saw the hot iron sizzling against Quin's chest – they saw how his fists clenched and his eyes seemed to scream their agony, and how, even then, he remained silent.

Lucius squirmed at every injury inflicted on his brother. He wanted to hide his eyes, run away, but he couldn't – not when Quin was unable to. Never before had he seen a display so mad, so heroic.

The crowd, who had loudly celebrated the under-trainers' intervention at first, now fell silent. They had seen in previous contests that Quin could fight and kill – they could not doubt his courage. It could not be faintheartedness that was motivating him now, but something far more noble. This determination to endure the pain of fire and flagellation for the love of his friend was yet further proof of the greatness of his soul. No wonder the gods had preserved him at

Pompeii. Cautiously at first – knowing that this could be interpreted by the authorities as an act of open rebellion – a few began to boo the under-trainers. Others quickly joined the cause, and soon half the stadium was openly jeering the officials.

Confused, and fearful of sparking a riot, the under-trainers turned for guidance to the imperial box. Lucius looked up towards the emperor, and was surprised to see that he wasn't there. His seat was empty. However, others in authority were present, including the consul, the praetor, the aediles and the Master of the Games. All were watching, but no one appeared willing to offer leadership. They were paralysed: as scared of upsetting the mob as they were of approving the outrageous behaviour of the gladiators. Eventually Ravilla rose from his seat – even though he had no formal authority at the games – and pointed at Trebellius. 'Beat him until he fights!' he screamed above the baying of the masses.

The under-trainers immediately ceased their attacks on Quin, and turned their attention back to Trebellius. The cracks of the whip on his flesh echoed horribly around the stadium, but – luckily for the under-trainers – did not seem to stir up the same level of outrage in the audience. The mob quietened, as the man from Calabria, lacking Quin's fortitude, cried out in agony. Stifling sobs, and with tears coursing down his cheeks, he eventually picked up his sword and swung it dazedly at Quin. He missed, and the momentum of the swing caused him to stagger and fall to his knees.

In response to a nod from Ravilla, the under-trainers again went to work on him, placing fresh cuts upon the earlier ones until his back became one great open wound. At last, when Quin could bear it no longer, he knelt down next to Trebellius and pulled his friend's face up from the ground so that he could look him in the eyes. Quin whispered something to him. Trebellius scarcely seemed conscious. Had he even heard what Quin had said? No one would ever know, because straight after that, Quin unsheathed his dagger and stabbed Trebellius through the heart.

Silus, still fuming over his humiliation in the arena, seemed determined to punish Lucius by working him as hard as possible. Lucius spent the rest of the afternoon feeding animals, mucking out cages and, worst of all, helping the butchers in the spoliarium. The light was already draining from the sky by the time he emerged, exhausted, his tunic soaked in animal blood, from the Hypogeum. He washed as best he could in a fountain, then headed over to the gladiator school to see Quin.

He found his brother in the medical room, lying on his side, head propped up on one elbow. A large bandage covered the burn on his chest. Quin's face was wincing with pain and his shoulders were shaking.

An exasperated Eumenes, the school's chief physician, was crouched behind him, tending to the carnage of his back.

'Stay still, will you!' cried Eumenes. 'Ah! Lucius! I could do with your help over here. Can you hold your brother while I apply these dressings.'

Lucius took hold of Quin's shoulders and tried to keep them still. He watched Eumenes take strips of wool that had been soaking in a bowl of honey-coloured liquid, and press them into the raw, blistering flesh.

'A mixture of deer rennet and vinegar to clean the wounds,' murmured Eumenes.

Quin sucked in a sharp breath at the sting of the vinegar, as another of the strips of wool was pressed home. 'I want to die,' he groaned.

'If that mob in the cheap seats hadn't come to your rescue, you'd have got your wish,' said Eumenes drily.

'What were you trying to achieve out there?' Lucius asked him.

Quin craned his neck and looked up at him through pain-fogged eyes. 'We agreed…' he said with a grimace. 'Trebellius and I agreed to fight, but not to kill each other.'

'But…'

'But nothing! We knew what would happen…' Quin arched his back as a fresh bolt of agony coursed through him, and Lucius was forced to tighten his grip on Quin's shoulders. 'We knew we'd be tortured, and we were prepared for it. I don't... I don't blame Ravilla. He did what he had to do. After your stunt with the elephant, I thought that maybe... maybe Titus, if he'd been there, would have shown us mercy. But only the emperor would have that kind of authority. When I saw he wasn't there, I knew...' He sucked in his breath with a hiss. 'I knew we were done for... They would have beaten Trebellius to death. I had to end his suffering – but as long as I live I'll carry a scar on my heart for what I did, worse than any on my body.'

'What did you say to him at the end?' asked Lucius.

'That's between me and Trebellius.'

'And what will happen to you now?'

'I don't know and I don't care.'

'What will happen,' broke in Eumenes, as he brushed a sponge gently over Quin's back, 'is that you'll receive an official pardon.'

'How do you know that?' asked Lucius.

'They have no choice,' said the physician. 'The mob will demand it. If the authorities don't pardon you, Quintus, they'll have a full-scale riot on their hands. The entire mess is their fault anyway. They should never have made you fight someone from your own school, let alone a friend. It's their mistake, and they'll have to clear it up.'

'What *is* that on the sponge?' asked Quin drowsily. 'That feels really good.'

'It's soaked in the juice of a poppy,' said Eumenes. 'It should dull the pain.'

A short while later, a slave came in carrying a jug of steaming liquid. He set it down on a table next to Quin's bed.

'Ah! Thank you!' said Eumenes. 'Boiled bark of elm. That should help close up the wounds.' He used a fresh sponge to apply the decoction.

The following evening, after finishing his duties at the amphitheatre, Lucius returned to the school. He found Quin on his own, resting on a bench under the colonnade that surrounded the great quadrangle. The bandages that swathed his torso were visible beneath his tunic.

'Hello, brother,' said Quin weakly. 'Did you have a good day at the slaughterhouse? I could hear the crowds from here. I could almost smell the blood.'

There was a hard, cynical look on Quin's face, masking a deeper sorrow. Lucius sat down next to him. The quadrangle was empty, but for a few slaves tidying away the training equipment. Angry purple clouds hung in the yellowing sky. They looked like burns, Lucius thought, and an image came to him of a firebrand hitting flesh.

'Trebellius told me once that Calabria is beautiful,' remarked Quin. 'One day, I'd like to go there.'

Lucius nodded indulgently. Then he noticed his brother was quietly sobbing.

'I'm glad I got branded!' he suddenly roared in misery. 'I don't know if it's a badge of honour or shame, but it's a reminder I'll carry with me… of the day I…' He collapsed, unable to continue.

Lucius stared at him, alarmed. Tentatively, he touched his shoulder. 'One of you had to die yesterday,' he said. 'That's just the way it goes. You can't blame yourself. You're a gladiator.'

'I don't feel like a gladiator any more.'

'I thought it meant everything to you.'

'Let's just say my eyes have been opened,' muttered Quin. He seemed calmer now, resigned. 'The Christians – they disapprove of the games, you know, Lucius. They call them barbaric. Trebellius told me about the Christians. Maybe they have a point…' He stopped talking as Crassus, the school's craggy-faced lanista, joined them on the terrace.

'Ah, Lucius!' he said, in his gruff but not unfriendly manner. He handed Quin a cup. 'Goat's milk with a pinch of cow dung, vinegar and honey. Compliments of Eumenes.'

Quin sniffed at it, and gagged.

'It's medicinal,' Crassus assured him. He took a seat on the bench. 'I bring good news, my friend. You're to receive an official pardon.'

Just as Eumenes predicted, thought Lucius.

'All being well,' continued the lanista, 'we can fix up another fight for you in two weeks' time. You're sure to have healed by then. And I've been promised it won't be with anyone from this school.'

'I'm not fighting,' said Quin quietly.

Crassus did not appear to hear him. 'Your most likely opponent is a Secutor by the name of Petronax, from the Claudian School. Eminently beatable, so my spies inform me. He favours first and second parries, but probably won't vary them...'

'I'm not fighting,' Quin repeated.

'What are you talking about?' frowned Crassus.

'I don't want to be a gladiator, Crassus. I resign.'

Crassus nodded solemnly, as if Quin's assertion merited serious consideration. 'You resign. I see.' He stood up so that his bulky shadow enveloped most of the bench, and he jabbed a finger at Quin's bandaged chest. 'What about the blood oath? Hm?' he shouted. '"I will endure to be burned, to be bound, to be beaten, and to be killed by the sword." Have you forgotten the vow you made?' He turned his pointing finger west, towards the amphitheatre. 'What about the fact that every day sixty thousand people scream your name from the terraces? What about the fact that the *emperor*, no less, has been asking after you and wondering when you might be fighting again?'

Quin didn't reply.

'Don't talk to me about resigning,' said Crassus. 'You've had a crisis of confidence. Sure, I can appreciate that. I've seen it before, lots of times. Usually happens after the first fight – for you it's come a little later... I know how much that boy meant to you. But he's gone now. Forget him! Remember who you are, Quintus Felix. Remember what you're here for, and what you mean to all the thousands who queue up every day to see you.' He headed for the door that led back inside. 'You start your training in two days!' Crassus marched away down the corridor.

'Are you serious about this?' asked Lucius.

Quin nodded. 'I can't fight again, not after what happened yesterday. When Trebellius died, so did all my love for this life.'

A feeling of relief mixed with fear suffused Lucius when he heard this. He had his brother back at last – the one he remembered from the time before the gladiatorial mania had taken him over. On the other hand, if Quin didn't fight, he was breaking his oath, and the punishment for that was death.

CHAPTER VIII

7 MARCH TO 1 MAY

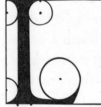ucius reckoned that if ever his brother needed his support, it was now. So each evening, instead of heading home, he made his way over to the gladiator school. It was soon clear that a crisis of major proportions was building there, all centred on Quin. Lucius could sense it in the hushed atmosphere in the corridors, and in the urgent, whispered conferences that he sometimes overheard behind half-open doors. He saw it in the uneasy looks on the faces of Crassus and the other trainers and under-trainers. Even Ravilla, whom he occasionally glimpsed striding through the main hall, seemed oppressed with unnameable anxieties.

It was hard to get to see Quin himself these days,

because he always seemed to be holding court with the administrators of the school or the officials in charge of the games. His star had risen so high in recent times that he'd been offered his own room at the school, and this now became an unofficial meeting room for the many who came to plead with him. Lucius would wait patiently in the corridor outside for them to emerge, and could always tell from their scowls of disappointment that they had failed once again in their mission of persuasion.

'I'm the star of the Inaugural Games, apparently,' Quin remarked to him nonchalantly one evening after one such meeting. 'And the fact that I refuse to compete has thrown everyone into such a tizzy. They dare not kill me – in fact, the emperor has expressly forbidden it – so they've started making these absurd offers. Hundreds of denarii for just a single appearance.'

'Aren't you tempted?' asked Lucius, thinking how such a purse could transform their lives – assuming Quin was willing to share it with his family.

Quin shook his head. 'I've vowed to myself never to kill another innocent man for sport – not for all the silver in Hispania.* I owe that much to Trebellius.'

'Then there's nothing they can do,' said Lucius happily. 'Eventually the games will end, and then they'll have to leave you alone.'

---

* *Hispania: the Roman name for the Iberian peninsula – present-day Spain, Portugal and neighbouring territories. It gave the Romans many valuable minerals, especially silver.*

When Lucius got home each evening, he always found Caecilia and Valeria waiting for him in the living room, eager for news of Quin. They managed to pick up scraps of gossip from the gladiator-school slaves who came to the fullery every day with their baskets of dirty laundry, but they relied on Lucius for a more detailed and accurate account of what was going on.

'The foolish boy!' Caecilia cried when Lucius first told them of Quin's refusal to fight. She wrung her cleaning cloth in a gesture of helpless frustration – she had been dusting when Lucius came in. 'He must know this can't end well for him.'

'I think he's brave,' said Valeria.

'And what do you know of bravery, my girl?' snapped Caecilia. 'Bravery is doing your duty, no matter what your personal feelings. He's a dreamer, that's what he is. Success has gone to his head, and now he thinks he's better than everyone else. He's not so different from his father in that respect. And now I fear that Quintus, too, will meet a sorry end.'

Apart from these regular arguments about the rights and wrongs of Quin's stand-off with the authorities, life at home continued fairly peacefully. Caecilia, it turned out, had very much enjoyed her evening at the house of Gordianus the tailor – though, to Lucius's great relief, she had not formed any kind of romantic attachment to the man. Still, that evening marked the beginning of a new social life for her. Gordianus had a small circle of friends in neighbouring insulae, and they often met in each other's apartments for evenings of games and conversation, to which Caecilia was always invited.

Valeria continued to spend her evenings with Euphemia and Simio down in the courtyard, while Lucius often visited Agathon and Argos. Agathon usually had an interesting new scroll to show him – a book on history, geography or natural philosophy that he'd managed to obtain from the scriptorium where he worked. For Lucius, these were treasures richer than diamonds. To his great delight, Agathon would sometimes lend one to him. Lucius would take the book home to his bed and very soon he'd be whisked away as if by magic to distant places and times.

Late one evening, after returning from a visit to Agathon with a brand-new scroll under his arm, Lucius lit his oil lamp and reclined on his bed. The book he had with him, the work of a Jewish historian by the name of Flavius Josephus, was a history of the Jewish–Roman War of ten years earlier. It didn't take him long to become absorbed in the narrative. Perhaps an hour into his reading, a particular passage relating the destruction of the Jewish temple in Jerusalem caught his eye. He reached over to his bedside table for his stylus and wax tablet, intending to make some notes. To his surprise, both were gone.

A few days later, while Lucius was over at Agathon's flat, playing on the floor with Argos, Agathon reminded him of the game of duodecim scripta, or twelve lines, which they used to enjoy. 'I still have that set at home,' said Lucius. 'I'll bring it next time I come over.' But when he returned home, he discovered that his board, dice and black and white counters were all missing.

The following evening, Caecilia called out to Lucius from the kitchen: 'Run down to Calenus the fishmonger and buy me some mullet, will you? You'll find some coins on the side table. And don't forget to smell it to make sure it's fresh before you pay him!' The coins weren't there. Nor was the leather pouch full of sestertii that he'd left on a chair in his room.

Over the next few days, a pair of sandals and a belt also vanished from Lucius's room. Worse by far, however, was the disappearance of the chalcedony ring Aquila had given him. This had become a talisman for Lucius, and the last tangible connection with his father. With its loss, he felt the goddess Fortuna had finally deserted him. Lucius embarked on a desperate search of the apartment. He was in Caecilia and Val's room, peering inside a trunk full of odds and ends, when he heard a scuffling sound coming from just outside the doorway. There was no one at home: Caecilia was out with her friends; Val was in the courtyard. It had to be the thief!

He leapt to his feet and ran into the living room just in time to see a hairy brown hand disappearing over the balcony ledge. Racing to the window, he caught sight of Simio bouncing off Calva's awning and landing lightly on all fours in the street. In his teeth was another of Lucius's prize possessions: his ankus. He watched the thieving chimp rise to his hind feet and embark on a lurching, weaving run across the road and down the alley that led to the courtyard.

So *that* was the talent that Val had been busy teaching him!

Simmering with indignation, Lucius ran downstairs, across the street and into the courtyard. He found Val patting Simio on the head and feeding him a fig as he handed over the ankus. Euphemia was also there, smiling proudly at the chimp as if he were a star pupil.

There, piled up in an old onion basket on the ground next to them, were Lucius's leather money pouch, sandals, belt and twelve lines set. The chalcedony ring was on Val's finger. His stylus and wax tablet were in her hands.

'I know what you're thinking,' Val said quickly to him. 'I know this looks bad.'

'You're training Simio to steal my stuff!' Lucius's anger echoed like a whipcrack around the insula walls. 'Of course it looks bad! It *is* bad!'

'I'm sorry,' said Val, biting her lip. She looked close to tears.

Euphemia, misjudging the mood, grinned and

said: 'But you have to admit, Lucius, he's a first-class housebreaker, isn't he?'

Lucius turned on her, making a huge effort to suppress the violent words that were struggling to break out of him. 'Yes. First-class,' he said coldly. 'And now I understand what your plans for him are. He was never going to *entertain* the crowds in the Forum, was he? You wanted him to *steal* from them!'

The girls' expressions of shock at this suggestion appeared genuine – but Lucius couldn't be sure if they weren't just good liars.

Val? A liar? There'd been a time not so long ago when such an idea would have seemed inconceivable. She used to tell him all her thoughts and secrets. But Suburra had changed her – she'd become harder, more closed to him, more devious.

During the tense silence that followed Lucius's accusation, Simio started using the ankus as a large drumstick, beating the sides of the cages and frightening the other animals in Euphemia's menagerie. Angrily, Lucius tried to wrench it from the chimp's grasp. Unfortunately, Simio assumed this was a new game, and tugged it back again with surprising strength. The battle of wills was eventually resolved by Val, who made a hand signal to the chimp. Simio let go of the ankus, and was rewarded with a fig. Contentedly chewing on this, he leapt over the cages and went swaggering off around the courtyard like a monarch on a tour of his kingdom.

Lucius's eye was drawn to the tablet on Val's lap. A long, thin object had been sketched in the wax. The object resembled his ankus.

He stared at Val, waiting for an explanation.

'I draw the object,' she said sheepishly, 'and then he goes off and steals it. This is the trick we've been teaching him... But Lucius, I was never planning to keep your stuff. I was going to give it back to you, honest!'

'Just tell me why you're doing this,' Lucius demanded.

Val looked about to say something, then she changed her mind. She bowed her head and wouldn't look at him.

'It's a stunt we're planning,' said Euphemia. 'First we'll work up a crowd in the Forum by getting Simio to do a few tricks – you know, a bit of balancing or juggling or something. Then, when a few people have gathered round, we'll ask a volunteer to describe something they've got hidden in their robes or their shopping basket. Val will draw it on the tablet, Simio will look at it, and then go and find it on the volunteer. That was our plan. Nothing dodgy, we promise!'

Lucius studied the two girls. He wasn't sure whether he believed Euphemia. If all they'd been doing was training Simio for a simple street trick to amuse the crowds, then why hadn't they said so straight away? Hadn't Val been about to confess to something serious just now, before Euphemia came up with her explanation?

Valeria handed Lucius back his ring and the basket of his possessions. 'We promise we won't steal from you ever again!' she said, with an attempt at an innocent smile.

They were definitely up to something, Lucius decided, and it was far from innocent.

One week after the confrontation in the courtyard, a fresh disaster struck the Inaugural Games. Carpophorus, the celebrated Bestiarius, was killed in the arena by a lion, and, with no sign of a return from Quintus Felix, the games were suddenly bereft of superstars. Demand for tickets tumbled; great swathes of seating remained empty each day. The organisers frantically tried to come up with new stunts to entice the crowds back. They paired rhinos with bulls, fixing metal spikes to their horns for added gore. They armed baboons with javelins and tried to get them to fight each other. They organised mock chariot races with monkeys driving wooden carts. But the laughter and cheering these desperate entertainments elicited was thin and scattered.

Political pressure grew on the organisers. The emperor wanted it known that he was not pleased. These games were being held to honour the memory of his imperial father, and they simply *had* to be a success. More hasty meetings were called, many of them going on late into the night. It was at one such conclave that someone made a suggestion that was to prove the salvation of the games. Later, no one could quite agree on who had made it – though many, including Ravilla, laid claim to the honour – but whoever it was, he was to earn the undying gratitude of everyone in Rome, from the lowliest freedman to the emperor himself.

The suggestion was this: we now have a vacancy for a Bestiarius. If Quintus Felix refuses to fight humans, why not get him to fight animals? Let him retrain as a Bestiarius.

By this time a month had passed since Trebellius's death. Quin's wounds had healed well, and his bitterness had eased somewhat. Although he remained steadfast in his refusal to fight as a gladiator, some of his old appetite for glory had returned. So the proposal that he should reinvent himself as a Bestiarius could not have been better timed. It offered him the chance to prove himself once more as a great fighter in the arena, without backing down on his pledge never again to shed innocent human blood.

The Bestiarii underwent their training at the Ludus Matutinus, or Morning School, so called because, at the games, the animal fights always took place in the mornings. The Morning School was situated about a hundred paces to the south on the same enormous square as the Ludus Romanus and the Flavian Amphitheatre. Like the gladiator school, the Morning School was a rectangular building with an open court in the middle where the men could practise. Around the court ran a roofed passage with rooms opening off it. As well as cells and dormitories, there was a kitchen, a dining hall, a medical room, an armoury, quarters for trainers and guards, a cemetery and a prison, complete with leg irons, shackles, branding irons and whips. And of course there were the animals...

One whole side of the school was taken up with cages and pens filled with aggressive beasts: bulls, bears, lions, tigers, leopards, cheetahs, wild boars, wolves and hyenas. They were specially reared for training Bestiarii, but most were ultimately destined for the arena. Silus often sent Lucius to the Morning School during the quieter afternoon periods, when the gladiator shows were on, to help feed these animals. As a result, Lucius had become quite friendly with the school's chief lanista, Ramio, whom he and Isi had first met during their guided tour of the Hypogeum. One afternoon in early April, Lucius saw Quin undergoing a training session with Ramio.

A leopard and a bull had been tied together by a long rope, with each end attached to one of their hind legs. Quin stood facing them about halfway in between, with a spear in his hand. Behind the tethered animals was Ramio, also armed with a spear, which he used to goad them towards Quin. As they advanced towards him, Quin gradually backed off. The leopard slunk low to the ground as it moved. Its movements were purposeful – it was definitely stalking Quin – but it was hampered by the drag on its rope-bound leg. The bear seemed less interested. It was moving towards Quin only because Ramio kept prodding it and because it was being pulled in that direction by the leopard.

'The rope restricts each animal's movement,' shouted Ramio as he egged them on. 'If I were to let one of them free now, you wouldn't stand a chance. Like this, you'll have time to dodge and defend yourself.'

Gradually, the bear began to show more interest in Quin. It shambled towards him and the rope slackened. The leopard seized the opportunity and darted forwards. Quin recoiled, lost his footing and fell backwards to the ground just as the leopard, with stunning swiftness, sprang at him, jaws wide. At the last second, the rope snapped taut, and the leopard fell awkwardly just short of Quin, its bound leg stretched out flat behind it. The bear, thankfully for Quin, had been diverted by the appearance of a female of its own species at the bars of a nearby cage.

Ramio raised Quin to his feet as if he were a small rabbit. The lanista was a huge man with bulging muscles. His vast head, thick neck and wide-spaced, watchful eyes gave him the appearance of a bull, and indeed that had been his nickname during his fighting days. The three parallel scars deeply etched into his cheek were both a badge of honour for him, and a constant reminder to his pupils of the very real dangers they faced.

'You're not big enough to be a Venator, as I was,'

he told Quin. 'But normally you're quick, at least – I've seen enough of your fights to know that. So why couldn't you dodge the leopard?'

'I don't know,' mumbled Quin.

Because it was too quick, even for him, thought Lucius as he fed a bowl of shoots and berries to the she-bear who'd saved Quin's life. *Quin would never admit it, but he simply wasn't fast enough.*

'I wasn't expecting it,' said Quin eventually.

'You've got to understand animal thinking,' said Ramio. 'They don't think like us. For one thing, you gladiators always get more time. There's this moment of hesitation before you go in for a kill. I call it the 'blink moment'. See, we humans are not natural killers – not many of us, anyway – so we have to tell ourselves to do it, and that slows us down. With animals, there's no blink moment. They operate purely on instinct. And if you're going to fight them, you've got to learn to think like them.'

As the days went by, Lucius watched as Ramio put Quin through his paces, teaching him the tricks of the trade. He taught him how to confuse a lioness by throwing a cape over her head, and how to fight a bear with a veil in one hand to distract the animal, and a sword in the other to dispatch it. At first, older and weaker animals were used in these exercises, but as Quin's technique improved, younger, fitter creatures took their places.

After two weeks, Ramio repeated the roped-animal

trick, and this time Quin passed it with ease, anticipating the leopard's leap a second before it came and then unleashing his spear. He deliberately missed with the spear – animals were expensive, and their blood was rarely spilt in the training arena. Ramio taught Quin how to goad animals to attack him by going very close and then retreating. And when he wasn't goading or fighting animals, Quin practised spear-throwing against a wooden target, or wrestled with Ramio. For these bouts, Ramio would don a pair of arm-length lion-fur gloves, complete with sharply clawed paws, to give Quin a sense of how it would feel to be at close quarters with a giant jungle beast.

For his next big challenge, Quin was faced with an unroped wild boar, which he successfully goaded to charge at him. The boar was both fast and aggressive – more so than Quin or maybe even Ramio expected. Quin was supposed to vault over a low fence to safety, but he mistimed it and received a tusk wound to the thigh that kept him off training for four days.

After a further week of daily training, Quin was exposed to two animals at once – a cheetah and a wolf – and he managed to evade them both. Then he was forced to lie on the ground while a bull was set on him. He was able to leap to his feet at the final instant to avoid its horns.

Lucius was amazed at his brother's progress. Even when Quin had performed his extraordinary dance-like fight with Trebellius, he'd never moved with such lightning swiftness, such supple, loose-limbed grace. He appeared to Lucius these days like a chimaera* of panther and snake as he prowled the training arena, limb muscles gleaming, poised for sudden movement, head jutted forwards, eyes needle-bright, spear arm raised, the spear's shaft grazing his cheek.

Even Ramio was starting to look impressed. 'You're doing OK, gladiator boy,' he said one afternoon. 'I do believe you're getting the hang of this. There's just one final challenge, and that's the subita incursio – the surprise attack. I can't teach you this one – you'll have to work it out for yourself.'

'What do you mean?' asked Quin.

Ramio just grinned. 'There are thirty-six trapdoors hidden beneath the arena sand, and the thing that wants to eat you could spring out of any one of them. There'll be trees and bushes all over the place obscuring your vision. The beast will see you long before you see *it*. You may only get a second, if that, to react.'

Ramio couldn't re-create the effect in the training arena, and didn't bother trying. 'It's not something you can ever rehearse,' he said cheerfully, 'so what's the point in killing yourself trying? No one ever remembers a Bestiarius who died in the Morning School. You and your reputation will live or die by this one event. Everything I've taught you will help you, sure. But it's ultimately down to you and whatever

---

* *chimaera: a mythical beast which was a combination of different animals.*

161

primitive instinct you have inside that will help you survive. If you *do* survive, and kill the beast, your name will live forever. Carpophorus managed it, as did I and a handful of others. But Carpophorus tried to go one better – he wanted to be the first to survive the subita incursio twice, and the second time, the lion killed him.'

'He was a fool,' said Quin with an admiring smile.

'Be that as it may,' said Ramio, his death has left us with a gaping hole in our morning shows, and everyone thinks that you are the man to fill it. I had my doubts at first, but now I'm starting to believe they may be right...'

CHAPTER IX

1–31 May

Quin did not disappoint Ramio. Over the next two weeks, he electrified the amphitheatre crowds with a series of spectacular feats. Armed only with a spear, he fought and slayed a male aurochs – a particularly fierce breed of wild, long-horned bull. He then evaded the charge of a one-tonne rhinoceros, before whipping around and dispatching it with a sword. Finally, he bested a Caledonian brown bear far taller than himself, notorious for having killed six previous Bestiarii. Quin received a shoulder wound for his trouble, but managed to kill the bear with his dagger.

'Your next task will be to avenge Carpophorus's death,' Ramio told Quin shortly after the bear fight.

The lanista was visiting him in the medical room, where Eumenes (whom Quin had insisted on bringing with him to the Morning School) and Lucius were busy patching up his latest wound.

'You mean I must kill the lion that killed him?' said Quin. Lucius was impressed by the steadiness of Quin's voice as he said this. Everyone had heard the tales of the Mesopotamian* Lion, as it had come to be known: that it had been bred since cubhood on a diet of human flesh, and now would eat nothing else – some said it would even charge through a herd of sheep just to get at the shepherd. Since Carpophorus's death, a new crop of legends had sprouted about the beast, to rival those surrounding the famous Nemean Lion killed by Hercules. Its fur was so thick, apparently, that it could withstand a sword's bite, while its teeth were sharp enough to cut through any armour.

'Not only must you kill this lion,' said Ramio, 'you must face it under the same circumstances as did Carpophorus.'

'The subita incursio,' murmured Quin.

The arena had been transformed into an African jungle – or the architect-engineers' idea of what a jungle should be. It was convincing enough, since

---

* *Mesopotamian: coming from the area between the rivers Tigris and Euphrates, which is roughly equivalent to present-day Iraq.*

few, if any, in the crowd were ever likely to see one for real. In truth, the landscape resembled a typical Italian forest, with thickets of oak, maple, holly, pine and cypress. The trees were interspersed with grassy glades and streams filled with water pumped in from the great aqueduct, the Aqua Claudia. The weather, at least, was appropriately African. The sun blazed out of a clear blue sky, and there was a hazy shimmer in the air above the forest. The spectators were, of course, shaded by the velarium, and their hot heads were further soothed by sparsiones – mist scented with balsam, sprayed from tiny holes in the walls at the rear of each section of terraced seating.

No such refreshing balm was available to Lucius and Isidora, however. They had spent the first part of the morning in the ovenlike conditions of the Hypogeum, loading trees and bushes into elevators for transport to the surface. Now, having finished these backbreaking chores, they sneaked upstairs to the equally hot, crowded room under the stands. They jostled their way past the other off-duty labourers to grab a position at one of the small, iron-barred viewing windows set into the perimeter wall. They were both filthy with mud, sweat and wood shavings, yet couldn't help but feel a swelling of pride as they gazed out upon their handiwork. Mingled with this for both of them, but especially for Lucius, was a deep sense of foreboding.

The stage was now set for Quin's fight with the

Mesopotamian Lion, and there wasn't an empty seat to be found in the amphitheatre – not even in the imperial box, where the emperor sat forward in his seat, looking as eager as any to witness this climactic contest between the two biggest stars to emerge from the games. Outside, the ticketless gathered in huge numbers in the great square. Though unable to witness the action directly, they were at least close to it, and could try to interpret, from the sounds of the lucky thousands inside, how things were going for their hero. Few, except his most diehard supporters, gave Quin much of a chance. Whatever his strengths as a gladiator, expert opinion agreed that he simply didn't have the strength or experience as a Bestiarius to defeat the animal that had killed the great Carpophorus. In fact, the betting stalls were refusing to take wagers on Quin's defeat, only on the question of how long he would last. The organisers were not too worried: the games were nearing an end anyway. Above all, they wanted a story that would ring down the ages, so that in centuries hence, when people spoke of the Inaugural Games, they'd recall the day Quintus Felix met the Lion of Mesopotamia.

'He's confounded expectations before,' said Isi reassuringly. 'Who knows, he might spring a surprise.'

'The only thing that's going to spring a surprise is the lion,' said Lucius bleakly. 'Look how many trees there are out there – it could jump out at him from behind any one of them.'

Lucius had tried to help his brother by surreptitiously hacking away some of the lower leaves and branches while Silus wasn't looking. But these efforts, he knew, were pitiful. He'd not seen the lion himself, but he'd heard its roars echoing through the Hypogeum while he was working that morning, and their volume and depth had sent rivulets of ice running through him, despite the heat. He'd heard rumours that they fed the beast with the remains of dead gladiators and executed criminals, but it had received nothing for three days now, and was ravenous.

Lucius's only hope lay in a deep-seated and entirely irrational belief in his brother – the same belief that had driven him to persuade others to disinter Quin from the rockfall that had buried him in Pompeii. An idea had grown in him that Quin was destined for greatness, and that this day was but one more stage in his journey.

Quin emerged, together with his arms-bearer, from the Gate of Life. He raised his hand to acknowledge the frenzied cheering from all sections of the stadium. Since his self-reinvention as a Bestiarius, his popularity had grown still greater, infecting even those who had despised him for his rebellion with Trebellius. Most believed that this would be his final fight, and their most fervent hope was that his death would be as great and glorious as the life that had preceded it.

Lucius watched nervously as Quin donned his helmet and shield and picked up his short sword. In his usual bold, unhesitating way, Quin stepped off the sand and into the fringes of the artificial forest. He moved slowly along a winding trail that led through the trees, head swivelling from side to side, sword raised in readiness. The thirty-six arena trapdoors were invisible – concealed beneath grass, earth, twigs and tree roots. Quin, like everyone else, could only guess at the timing and direction of the surprise attack.

This fight has come a day too early, thought Lucius sadly. *If Quin dies this morning, he'll never know that Father was innocent, nor that Ravilla, his beloved uncle, was the Spectre.* If all went well, they should have proof of this tonight. The plan had been laid. His mind returned briefly to the conversation he'd had with Val the previous evening…

'I have to tell you something,' Val had said, furtively entering Lucius's bedroom.

Lucius looked up from his book. 'Don't you believe in knocking?' he asked sternly.

His sister came and sat down next to him on his bed. 'There's something I've been keeping from you, and I'm sorry.'

'Is this about Simio?' He hadn't forgotten the confrontation they'd had two months ago, even though Simio appeared to have stopped his thieving ways since then.

Val nodded. 'Partly.' She swallowed. 'Phee and I weren't completely truthful with you that day about what we were doing... In fact we weren't truthful at all.'

Lucius could feel his indignation stirring at this, but she raised her hand in a placating gesture. 'Before you start getting all moral on me again, please hear me out. The thing we were training Simio for isn't exactly legal, I admit, and it's not without its dangers. I was also very unsure back then whether it was even possible. But it's something I think you'll approve of, once you hear what it is.'

Lucius sat up straighter. She'd certainly got his attention now. 'What in Hades are you talking about, Val? What are you planning?'

Val studied Lucius for a long moment, as if trying to work out whether she could trust him. Eventually, she said it: 'I know where Ravilla's letter is, and I want Simio to steal it for us.'

'What! Are you out of your mind? Where?'

'You remember that beautiful gold candelabrum?' she continued quickly. 'The one that Ravilla showed us, in his triclinium? He called it a Menorah.'

'Yes. What about it?'

'While I was holding it, I felt these bumps in the surface of the main stem. I looked closer and saw that it had a small door in it, like a door to a hidden compartment. Later, when we didn't find the letter in the red box, I remembered about the Menorah and

I thought to myself – wouldn't it be a perfect place to hide something in? Such as a letter he didn't want anyone to find!'

Lucius smiled at his sister as he realised that for all her recent signs of growing maturity, she was still really just a little girl, with a little girl's fanciful notions about life.

'That's a neat idea, Val,' he said, 'but think about it a moment, will you? Just suppose there *is* a secret cavity inside that candelabrum – why should that be where Ravilla chooses to hide the letter? There must be thousands of better places in that house. For example, while I was upstairs I saw a library with hundreds of scrolls. He could have hidden it inside any one of them, or at the bottom of a trunk, or who knows where else. Hiding it inside an object that's on public view in his triclinium seems the least likely possibility of all…'

'And therefore the *most* likely,' insisted Val. 'Don't you see, Lu? Because the Menorah is in plain sight, it's the last place anyone would think of looking for something so secret.'

'That's a fair point,' Lucius conceded. 'But still, I don't see why the letter should be there and not in a thousand other places.'

'There was something else,' said Val. 'When you came back into the room and Ravilla started talking to you, I took the opportunity to grab a closer look at that secret door in the Menorah. I saw a tiny symbol engraved on it.'

She reached for Lucius's stylus and wax tablet and began to draw. He gradually recognised her sketch as a crude rendition of a symbol he'd once seen long ago – and the sight of it made him shudder deep inside.

It was about two years ago, back in the days when they still lived in their grand house on the Esquiline Hill. One night, Lucius was awoken by the sound of urgent voices from below. Curious and a little scared, he crept downstairs and crouched in the shadows by the door of his father's study, or tablinum. His father was in there, speaking to a visitor, whom Lucius recognised as the well-known senator Marcus Cornelius Getha.

This was at the height of the so-called 'Terror', when the ageing emperor Vespasian had begun to grow paranoid about plots against him, and people were disappearing from public life almost every week. Getha looked like a ghost. His face was grey, his eyes dull, even in the flames from the fire. Lucius guessed that he must have been accused of treason. He had come to ask Aquila to plead his case, though, from the expressions of both men, Lucius guessed there was little that Aquila could do for him. In those days, being accused of treason was the same as being found guilty of it.

During the course of their conversation, Getha reached within the folds of his toga and drew out a letter. 'Pulcherius, the commander of the Praetorian Guard, showed me this tonight,' he said. 'It's a copy of a letter from an informer accusing me of being involved in the Sidonius conspiracy. I never even knew Sidonius – it's quite ridiculous!'

Aquila pointed at something on the letter. 'I've seen this before, on another letter,' he said quietly. 'It's the sign of the Spectre.'

'By the girdle of Medusa!'* breathed Getha. 'Then I am finished.'

Lucius crept closer. In the flickering light of a hanging oil lamp, he saw what his father had been indicating: at the bottom of the letter was a drawing of a bird in flight. It had the wing shape and tail fan of a kestrel – and an arrow through its heart.

The next morning, full of excitement at what he'd seen, Lucius had drawn the symbol and shown it to Valeria. Now, two years later, she was drawing the same symbol for him. 'It's the sign you showed me once,' she said. 'The sign of the Spectre.'

Lucius nodded gravely. The reappearance of the symbol scared him, but also gave him new hope. Val had almost certainly found the hiding place of the letter! He thanked Minerva, the goddess of wisdom, for Val's super-sharp eyes, and for the fact that they had even recognised the symbol – for there could not be many who had seen it and lived.

'Why have you waited so long to tell me this?' he asked her.

* *Medusa: one of the three gorgons in Greek mythology, a monstrous woman with snakes for hair.*

Val lowered her head. 'Because I want to keep you alive, Lu. I want at least *one* brother.'

'What are you talking about?'

'I knew what would happen. As soon as I told you about the Menorah, you'd start plotting ways to steal it. You'd get caught, Ravilla would realise that you know his most deadly secret, and he'd kill you for sure. I didn't want that to happen.'

Lucius gave a snort. Val was probably right to think he'd react that way, and her desire to protect him was endearing, but he was hurt by how little faith she had in his chances of success. 'So why are you telling me now?' he asked.

'I wanted to wait until I had an alternative plan – a plan that didn't involve you risking your neck. That plan is now finally ready.'

'You mean getting Simio to steal it?' said Lucius incredulously. 'You've got more confidence in that chimp than your own brother!' Despite his wounded pride, Lucius started to chuckle. He'd never heard of a more ridiculous scheme in his life. 'So *that's* why you started teaching him to steal things – you were prepping him for the big heist! But stealing a few things from my bedroom is hardly the same as breaking through locked doors and evading armed guards, is it? And how exactly were you expecting him to *find* the Menorah in that enormous house? Draw him a map?'

Val looked at her hands. 'I knew you'd react like this,' she said in a low, forlorn voice. 'That's another reason why I held off telling you for so long.' Then she raised her head and looked at him, and Lucius discerned a new determination in her hazel eyes. 'Come with me, brother,' she said. 'I want to show you something.'

Curious now, he followed her out of the room, down the stairs and into the street. It was a warm evening, teeming with shoppers, dawdlers and homebound market traders driving wagons full of their unsold wares, and it took a while to cross the busy thoroughfare. Val led him down the narrow alley into the quiet of the courtyard. The place had been transformed since he was last there. The menagerie was gone – or at least the animals were. The cages had been piled up haphazardly in the middle of the yard and a crude plaster sculpture of a leaping dolphin had been placed on top of them. A large hexagonal outline had been chalked around the pile of cages. Two winding parallel lines, also in chalk, had been drawn on the cobbles, passing alongside the cages and extending from one end of the yard to the other.

'What have you done here?' asked Lucius in amazement. 'Where are the animals?'

'Out earning their keep in the Forum,' called Euphemia from her first-floor balcony on the right-hand side of the courtyard. 'My dad rents them out to street entertainers – makes quite a decent income from it.' Simio was next to her, savouring an apricot as he perched regally on the balcony's balustrade.

'Have you told him, then?' Euphemia asked Val.

Val nodded. 'I thought it was time – now that we're confident Simmy can do it.'

'In that case we ought to give Lucius the full demonstration,' said Euphemia. She made a hand sign to the chimp, who immediately clambered over the side of the balcony, leapt lightly down to the cobbles and sidled up to Val.

She petted him affectionately on the head. 'We don't need to give Simmy a map,' Val explained to the bewildered Lucius. 'We've given him a replica of Ravilla's garden instead. Look! Those cages with the dolphin on top are the fountain in the hexagonal pool, and those winding lines are the gravel path, and Phee's balcony is the terrace leading to the triclinium – OK, I realise it's not exactly the same, but it's close enough for a creature as bright as Simmy, don't you think?'

Lucius observed her eager, shining eyes. She so wanted his approval! Still, his cautious nature saw only difficulties. 'How's he going to get into the garden?' he asked her. 'He's got to get past the heavily guarded door, the vestibule *and* the atrium.'

'He won't need to,' she said excitedly. 'Follow me.' She took Simio's hand and began walking back out of the alley. A mystified Lucius followed them. They turned a corner and walked a little way along the street until they were standing in front of the insula that backed onto the left-hand side of the courtyard. She gave Simio a hand signal, and the chimp immediately leapt at the wall. He began a rapid, graceful ascent, finding tiny chinks and handholds amid the brickwork, so that within a minute he had reached the roof.

'Quick!' said Val. 'Let's meet him when he comes down the other side. Lucius ran with her back up the alley in time to see Simio beginning his descent into the courtyard.

'You're sending him over the top of Ravilla's house?' gasped Lucius, finally getting it. 'You're a genius, Val!'

She smiled at him, thrilled to receive at last her brother's endorsement of her plan.

When Simio reached the cobbles, he immediately set off between the winding chalk lines, past the 'dolphin fountain' and then up onto Euphemia's balcony. Val and Lucius quickly ascended the staircase to the balcony in time to see Simio enter her living room and reach for a gold-painted replica of the Menorah placed in a recess at the far end of the room.

Lucius couldn't help but admire the immense efforts the girls had gone to for the sake of this project. Now he saw why it had taken so many weeks to set it up. He watched as Simio, Menorah in hand, hurdled back over the balcony before retracing his steps through the courtyard and up the wall at the far end.

'How have you explained all this to your father?' Lucius asked, suddenly concerned that the plan might leak back to Caecilia.

'Oh, to him it's all just a grand, crazy game we've created to amuse ourselves,' laughed Euphemia.

'He thinks I'm half bats anyway, so this is all perfectly in character!'

'What do you think, Lu?' asked Val anxiously.

Lucius watched as Simio came bounding triumphantly back into the alley, the fake Menorah held aloft in one hand, like a gladiator holding up his victory palm. When the chimp had returned to the balcony, Lucius handed him a fig from a bowl on the living-room table.

'I think we should do it,' he said.

Now, as Lucius watched his brother edge his way cautiously into the artificial forest, he rubbed his father's chalcedony ring, silently mouthing a prayer to Fortuna. Simio would make the snatch tonight. Quin had to survive, if only so that he could know the truth about his family's story.

The crowd watched expectantly as their hero penetrated deeper into the wood. The clumps of trees had been positioned with gaps between them, so that Quin would always remain visible to the spectators. His highly polished helmet and sword were bright beacons moving among the dull browns and greens of the vegetation. Barely a sound could be heard, but for the distant flap and creak of the velarium and the gentle hiss of the sparsiones with their scented spray. Where was the lion?

Suddenly, from out of the silence, there came a cry from someone in the upper seats: 'I see it!'

Everyone stood up, desperate to catch a glimpse of the legendary creature. More cries resounded, and fingers began pointing towards the northern side of the arena, beneath the imperial box. Lucius looked and saw a blur of something big and brown moving through the trees. It was approaching Quin very fast from his right.

'Watch out!' Lucius screamed, in unison with sixty thousand others.

Quin stopped and looked around. He was in a clearing near the middle of the arena. The lion was close now, but still invisible to him. For such a big creature, it was incredibly quiet. Lucius could only see parts of it until, for just a few seconds, it stepped through a glade and leapt a stream before passing back into the trees. For that brief moment, he saw the beast in full. It was bigger – much bigger – than he had anticipated. Its dark gold fur was scarred with a javelin wound at the top of its hind leg. A long, silky mane extended across its enormous head to its muscular shoulders and right across its belly.

The beast was now just a few paces from Quin, crouching low in the trees. Lucius could see only part of its head. It spread its mouth into a snarling gape, revealing a pair of long, curving yellow fangs.

This is not fair, thought Lucius, panicked. *It's too big!*

Too powerful! It has all the advantages of tree cover! What chance does Quin have?

Like everyone else in the stadium, Lucius was screaming at the top of his voice, trying to warn Quin where the animal was, but he realised that to his brother the noise of the spectators must sound like an incomprehensible roar.

The lion lowered its shoulders and raised its hindquarters, ready to spring; and still Quin had no idea which direction it was coming from – only that it was near. Then, with a violent swish of leaves and branches, the lion launched itself. It emerged from its hiding place like a golden bolt from a ballista,* claws out and teeth bared, ready to tear and chew its victim's flesh.

Quin had less than a second to react. In one movement, he twisted his body to face the lion, dropped to one knee and began raising his shield to receive the shock. But it was all too quick for him – the great beast struck him before he could get his shield into position. Quin was thrown back with such force, he hit his head at the base of a tree, stunning himself. The shield fell from his arm. To a groan of dismay from the crowd, the lion bit into Quin's left shoulder with its teeth and started to drag him back into the forest.

'Too soon!' came the cries of the crowd. 'We wanted a fight!' This was not the glorious contest they'd been hoping for. The emperor slumped in his throne. The

* *ballista: an artillery weapon resembling a giant crossbow.*

179

organisers quietly despaired – it was the last time they'd take Ramio's word about the 'brilliance' of one of his students.

Isidora grabbed Lucius's hand and pressed it hard. He bit his lip, forcing himself to watch to the bitter end. His brother was nothing if not resilient – if he could only regain consciousness in time. Helplessly, Lucius watched as the blood darkened Quin's tunic. The lion dragged its victim through some bushes and then through a stream.

The water seemed to rouse Quin at last. He raised his short sword and brought its blade down against the lion's side in a chopping motion, leaving a bloody gash in its fur. The beast roared in shock and pain, dropping Quin. It tried to pounce on him, but with extraordinary speed he rolled clear and jumped to his feet. Cheers exploded from the stands as he took a flying leap onto the lion's back and wrapped his arms around its neck. The lion twisted its head and snapped its jaws, but couldn't reach Quin. It started tearing through the forest, trying to shake him free. He half slid off so his lower legs were being dragged along the ground, but he clung on determinedly with his arms, squeezing the underside of the beast's neck with all his might.

With such a weight dragging it down on one side and a painful stranglehold on its throat, it was remarkable how long the lion managed to continue running, tossing and turning. Eventually, though, Quin's efforts forced it to collapse onto its side. As it fell, it twisted its head back and took a bite over its shoulder, ripping a slice from Quin's tunic. He leapt clear, now bare-chested, the bloody wound in his shoulder visible for all to see. The lion immediately spun around and struck Quin with its forepaws – left, right, like a boxer. Quin was knocked backwards, fresh claw wounds appearing on his chest and stomach. Before the lion could take advantage, Quin swiftly scrambled to his feet. His shield lay somewhere back near the path, and he tried to edge closer to it, but the lion circled back until it stood between the Bestiarius and his objective.

They were now a few paces apart, both bleeding from their wounds. From fifty paces away, behind the safety of the perimeter wall, the sight of the monstrous creature made Lucius sweat droplets of ice. What it must appear like to Quin, he didn't want to imagine. But if his brother was scared, he didn't show it. He looked his foe squarely in the eyes, sword raised, knees slightly bent. The lion emitted a deep roar that reverberated through the bones of every spectator. Yet it seemed hesitant – content to circle Quin, but making no advance on him. Quin began shouting hoarsely and waving his sword at the beast.

'He's trying to provoke a charge,' Lucius murmured to Isidora. During the final leap, the lion's underside would be exposed. If Quin moved fast enough, he might be able to roll underneath it and land a fatal blow. Lucius had seen enough of the training sessions to understand the strategy, though it seemed like an impossible manoeuvre with a creature as big and quick as this one. Quin swayed from side to side in front of the animal. He bashed the flat of his sword against a nearby tree, but still the lion refused to charge.

'Why can't he just run around the lion and go and get his shield?' Isidora asked.

'Turning your back on a creature like that is fatal,' said Lucius. 'With one bound, the lion will have him. His only chance is to try and goad it to attack.'

Quin's shoulder, chest and stomach were now covered in blood pouring from his wounds. Lucius could see his brother was weakening. His goading tactics had left him breathless and wobbly-legged. He was running out of time and options. The lion was salivating from the scent of fresh human blood, yet it seemed content to bide its time, waiting for its prey to falter or flee before moving in. The beast was clever as well as powerful.

To gasps of awe from the crowd, Quin decided to embark on what appeared a desperate scheme. He began edging *closer* to the lion. The beast snarled and licked its lips. When there were just three paces between them, Quin tore off a ragged piece of his tunic. He wiped his chest with it, smearing it with his blood. Then he held it out before him, just in front of the lion's nose.

Seeing this, Lucius's mouth went as dry as dead animal bones. One snap of those jaws, and Quin's arm would be gone. The lion seemed to throb with suppressed violence. It made a thick slurping sound and a fresh stream of drool leaked from its mouth. Quin waved the rag slowly in front of the lion, taunting it with the blood scent. The creature's jaws widened briefly to a snarl – then bit down on Quin's arm...

No!

The air was filled with screams of horror.

But wait... The entire crowd, including Lucius, had missed something. Quin's arm was still there! The lion's jaws had cracked down on air. Faster than eyes could see, Quin must have whipped his arm out of range. The lion, now maddened with frustrated hunger, coiled itself and vaulted towards him. Quin tried to duck, but the huge paws were already on his shoulders, pushing him down. Man and beast crashed to the earth, Quin pinned beneath its clawed feet, his face in biting distance of its jaws. Everyone waited for the mauling and tearing to begin. Many who'd witnessed the lion's previous bout were reminded of Carpophorus's final moments. They decided that Quin had given a better show against the Mesopotamian monster than even his celebrated predecessor had managed. What a waste – and such a young man, too!

Lucius held his breath. Why was the creature waiting? Something must have happened. Instead of moving in for the kill as expected, it gave a great shudder. Its breath rattled and then it simply lay there, slumped on top of Quin. Bewildered shouts and mutterings engulfed the terraces as people struggled to comprehend what had just happened. Finally, Quin scrambled out from beneath the beast. As he did so, the lion rolled onto its side, and then everyone saw the sword buried in its belly almost up to the hilt. They hadn't seen it go in – Quin had moved too fast. The Mesopotamian Lion was probably as shocked as everyone else to discover that it was dead.

Scattered cries of astonishment were swiftly taken up by others, gathering in pitch and volume until the entire stadium was shouting, singing and screaming their amazement at the miracle they had just witnessed. Surely, this man was touched by Jupiter himself. There was no question now – his feats were the stuff of legend. Nothing and no one could defeat him.

Lucius hugged Isidora in utter delight and amazement. 'He did it!' he cried, dancing with joy. Outside, on the terraces, a chant began, which soon echoed around the amphitheatre and the great square beyond: *Quintus Felix Rex! Quintus Felix Rex! Quintus Felix Rex!**

Wearily, Quin raised his hand in triumph. He got slowly to his feet and began to stagger along the path through the trees towards the Gate of Life. Long before he got there, he collapsed. Stretcher-bearers rushed to his aid. As he was carried off, he raised his arm once more to the adoring masses.

* *Quintus Felix Rex!: Quintus Felix is king!*

PART THREE

FIRE AND DAMNATION

CHAPTER X

31 MAY

'Curses on Luna,'* murmured Lucius, frowning at the big round moon hanging above them. He, Val and Simio were crouching within a screen of cypress trees on the Palatine Hill, just across the road from Ravilla's house. Moonlight bathed the road and the high white walls of the property, lighting up the scene more clearly than a hundred flaming torches.

'It's too bright tonight. He'll be seen.'

'We'll just have to risk it,' said Val. 'We're coming up to the second watch of the night. The guards can't be expecting anything to happen now.'

Simio was on his feet, shaking the cypress branches

* *Luna: goddess of the moon.*

and making little chattering noises in his throat.

'Can't you shut him up?' begged Lucius.

'He knows something's up,' whispered Val. 'He's just excited, like a child who's allowed out for the first time at night.'

Worried that they might be discovered, Lucius clamped a hand over Simio's babbling mouth. The chimp gave a little scream and nipped his finger.

'Ow!' yelped Lucius.

'That was silly of you,' chided his sister. 'You don't want to get him all upset just before the biggest moment of his life.' She cuddled the chimp and made soothing whispery noises into his ear. Then she took the fake Menorah from her bag and showed it to Simio. He tried to grab it, but she looked him in the eyes and shook her head. He followed her gaze as she turned to face the wall of Ravilla's house. She made a complicated series of hand signs that Lucius was at a loss to interpret, but Simio followed them all closely. Finally, she showed him a glimpse of some juicy figs she had in her bag: the reward!

Simio immediately set off, waddling across the road and then scrabbling his way up the rough stone wall. His dark, hairy figure stood out clearly against the white paint, but luckily no guards were around to see him. He leapt with extraordinary agility from one scarcely visible hand- or foothold to another, and within a minute he had reached the red-tiled roof. He clambered lightly up the tiles to the peak of the roof, where his shape was silhouetted by the moon. He crouched there hesitantly, looking around, as if uncertain of what to do next.

'He's confused,' groaned Lucius. 'He doesn't know where he's supposed to go.'

'Give him time,' said Val. 'He'll figure it out.'

A moment later he disappeared from view down the other side.

'He must have seen the dolphin statue down in the garden!' whispered Val excitedly. 'He'll be fine now!'

'Until he's spotted by a guard,' said Lucius. 'You didn't rehearse him for that eventuality, did you?'

'He won't be,' said Val blithely. 'No one will spot him, because no one would ever expect him. Whoever heard of a chimp thief?' She smiled. 'He'll be on the gravel path by now, making his way past the dolphin fountain... Now he'll be leaping up onto the terrace, and...'

She stopped, her face freezing into an expression of sudden anguish. 'Oh no!' she cried. 'Oh, Lu, I forgot about the window leading into the triclinium. Of course it would be closed up at night, wouldn't it? The shutters would be closed.'

Lucius stared at her, disappointment stealing over him like a shadow.

'I tried to think of everything,' wept Val. 'How stupid of me.'

'Never mind!' said Lucius, trying to think of something reassuring to say. 'Let's call this a practice run, shall we? We'll get Simmy working on his lock-picking skills in the morning, then next week we'll come back and try again!'

'Lock-picking skills!' said Val incredulously. 'Simmy may be clever, but even *you* must know that a chimp could never pick a lock.' She sniffed. 'I just have to accept that my plan was a failure. We'll have to think of something else.'

Lucius squeezed her shoulder. 'I think your plan was brilliant,' he said, 'despite its one fairly major flaw.' His smile was faintly teasing.

She elbowed him softly in the ribs.

'Ouch!' cried Lucius.

They waited in silence for Simio to return.

'Where *is* he?' wondered Val. 'He should have been back by now.'

Suddenly, the stillness of the night was rent by the shrill clanging of an alarm bell.

'Nemesis!' cursed Lucius. 'He's been discovered!'

Val moaned in fear. 'What shall we do?'

The clanging went on and on. From within the house they could hear shouts and running footsteps.

'If we're discovered here, they'll know we're responsible,' said Lucius, pulling Val further into the trees. 'The safest thing would be to make a run for it.'

'I'm not leaving Simmy,' insisted Val.

The front door opened and a red-liveried guard poked his head out. He carefully scanned the road in both directions. Lucius and Val froze, unsure whether they were visible. The guard stepped out of the house and walked slowly across the road towards them. He peered into the cypress trees where they were hiding. Could he see them? Lucius didn't breathe. He imagined himself made of stone. Val appeared equally motionless beside him. The bell continued its incessant clanging.

Eventually, the guard began to make his way back across the road towards the house. As he did so, Val gave a faint gasp and pointed towards the roof. Lucius looked up to see that Simio had reappeared there. Incredibly, he was clutching the gleaming gold Menorah in his fist.

'He did it!' she breathed. 'Oh, Simmy, you genius! But how?'

The guard looked up and saw him, too. He gave a great bellow: 'I see it! Come, quickly!' He ran to the front entrance and screamed for assistance. 'Bring spears! I've seen the intruder!'

Simio, clearly frightened by the shouting and the bell, clattered down the roof tiles and began a rapid descent of the wall. He lost his footing about halfway down and fell awkwardly to the road, spilling the Menorah. Lucius and Val ran over to him. Val picked him up in her arms and began sprinting down the street. Lucius reached to pick up the Menorah. As he did so, a spear thudded into the ground just a hand's breadth away. He jerked away in terror, then grabbed the Menorah and began running as fast as he could after Val. The thudding footsteps of the guards chasing them were like hammers pounding on his heart.

They rounded a bend in the road, and suddenly he could no longer see Val. He was about to run on, hoping she might be somewhere ahead, when he heard a scraping of stone to his left. In the shadows, the cover of an underground aqueduct seemed to be sliding open by itself. From the black space beneath the lid, he heard Val's hoarse whisper: 'Lucius! Quick! Jump in!'

Without thinking, Lucius did so. He landed with a splash in the water at the bottom of the pipe. Losing his balance, he fell backwards, getting himself thoroughly soaked. Then he stood up and cracked his head on the top of the pipe.

'Aarggh!' he groaned, his voice echoing in the confined space.

'Ssshhh!' hissed Val, hastily sliding the lid shut.

They crouched in the darkness, up to their knees in cold, sluggishly flowing water, listening to the sound of the guards' footsteps fading away.

'I was really hoping Ravilla wouldn't find out about this until morning,' whispered Lucius. 'I wanted to take this to the authorities before he even knew we'd stolen it.'

'Maybe the guards didn't see us,' said Val hopefully.

'Even if they didn't, we'll still be the first suspects on Ravilla's list. Don't forget, we were there the night his red box disappeared, and I think he may also have guessed that I overheard his conversation with Valens in Pompeii.'

'So what do we do?' wondered Val. 'We can't go home, can we?'

'No,' said Lucius firmly. 'I'm sure Ravilla's men will be on their way there right now. Our only hope is to take the Menorah to Agathon's flat and open it there. If all goes well and the letter is inside it, we can take it straight over to the Praetor's Office first thing tomorrow morning.'

They waited another ten minutes, then cautiously emerged from their underground hideout and began walking swiftly down the road, keeping to the shadows. Lucius carried the Menorah beneath his cloak, while Val walked hand in hand with Simio.

Lucius had mentioned their plans to Isi earlier that evening, and she had asked if she could join them when they opened the Menorah; so, before going to Agathon's flat in the Velabrum, they headed over to the gladiator school, where she was still living.

Despite the late hour, the square next to the amphitheatre was crowded with people. The embers of campfires glowed on the cobbles between the hide tents of ticketless fans. A crowd of revellers was milling around the entrance to the Morning School, singing songs and chanting *Quintus Felix Rex!* Lucius, Val and Simio sneaked past them – luckily, the revellers were too drunk to notice the chimpanzee.

They went to Isi's window in the slave quarters of

the Ludus Romanus, and Lucius whispered her name. Within seconds Isi appeared and began climbing out. She'd been waiting for them. She gasped at the sight of the Menorah.

'You did it!' she whispered excitedly. 'Is the letter in there?'

'We don't know yet,' said Lucius. Briefly, he explained what had happened, and their change of plan.

As they made their way back past the Morning School, a hunched figure shrouded in a hooded cloak hobbled up to them. At first, Lucius assumed it was an old man seeking alms. He opened his leather pouch to give him a coin, but then the old man spoke:

'Lucius! It's you, isn't it?'

Lucius stared into the shadowy depths of the hood and was amazed to see his brother in there.

'Quin!' cried Val delightedly.

'Sshhh!' he hushed her, looking nervously at the chanting crowd outside the school entrance. 'I'm trying to get away from these people. They've besieged the school, so I disguised myself and was in the middle of escaping when I saw you.'

'But shouldn't you be in the medical room?' asked Lucius. 'I mean, you *were* nearly eaten by a lion earlier today.'

Quin gave a derisive snort. 'I used to get more injuries in my play fights with Val,' he grinned, pinching his sister affectionately on the cheek. 'Actually, Eumenes would probably kill me if he knew I was up and about, but I was bored and full of energy, and I simply had to get out of there!'

Glancing around, he spotted Isi and the chimp. 'Why, Isidora! How nice to see you again... And a monkey! Is this your new pet, Val? My girl, you seriously need to update me on your life!' He smiled. 'It's so great to be around family and friends again! Bestiarii are not the most inspiring company, I can tell you! So anyway, where are you all off to at this late hour, and is there any chance I can tag along?' He looked at Lucius encouragingly, and Lucius stared back, unsure what to say.

'We're going to Agathon's flat to –,' Val began.

'To say hello,' Lucius swiftly interrupted, casting a stern look towards Val. She ought to know that Quin could not be trusted on this matter – not yet, anyway. Once he actually saw the letter, his attitude might change.

While visiting the gladiator school during Quin's recuperation there, Lucius had told Quin about his reacquaintance with Agathon, so Quin was not entirely surprised by their destination, only by the timing of their visit. 'It's a little late for a social call, isn't it? But hey-ho! It'll be nice to see my old pedagogue* again.'

As they made their way to Agathon's flat, Val plied Quin with questions about what it had been like to go up against the Mesopotamian Lion. Meanwhile,

* pedagogue: a slave who looked after a child's education. The name means 'child leader' in Greek.

Isidora updated Lucius with the latest news about Kato the tiger. Several weeks ago he'd been moved out of the Hypogeum into the fresher air and more spacious environment of the Morning School. Helped by these new surroundings, he was now fully recovered.

'That's good news, isn't it?' said Lucius, puzzled by Isi's sad expression.

'Yes and no,' she said. 'I'm thrilled he's better now, but also terrified, because it means he'll have to fight in the arena. Any day now, Silus is going to give the order. I can't bear it, Lucius. I mean I've got used to my animals dying – I've said goodbye to enough of them. But Kato – we've developed such a bond. I don't *want* to say goodbye to him.'

When they reached Agathon's flat, Argos gave them his usual hearty welcome at the top of the stairs. Quin was delighted to see the family dog again and proceeded to roll around with him on the floor of the narrow passageway until the dog placed a paw on his wounded shoulder, causing him to cry out in pain.

The commotion roused the sleeping Agathon, who came to the door in a hurry, wrapping his tunic around him, a smoky oil-lamp in his hand. When he saw who was there, he gave such a leap of surprise that he nearly knocked himself out on the lintel of his low doorway.

'Come in! Come in!' he cried. They all crowded into the tiny living room.

'Quintus!' exclaimed Agathon. 'How lovely! To

what do I owe this… Why, Lucius, what is that you have beneath your cloak?'

Lucius drew out the shiny gold Menorah.

'But it's beautiful. Wherever did you…?'

Quin grabbed it and held it up to Agathon's flame. 'Lu, this is stunning. Where did you get it?'

Lucius tensed. It was confession time. 'We got it from Ravilla,' he said.

'That's an extremely generous gift!'

Lucius took it from him and handed it to Val. In the candlelight, he watched her slender fingers search the central stem for the indentations.

'Here,' she whispered.

Lucius leaned close and made out the miniature door about halfway up the stem, between the first and second pairs of branches. Just as Val had said, engraved in the bottom corner was the tiny figure of a kestrel with an arrow through its heart – the mark of the Spectre!

Lucius swallowed. 'If we're right, we'll find a letter inside here.'

The lamp shook in Agathon's hand. '*The* letter?' he asked tremulously.

Lucius nodded.

'What are you talking about?' asked Quin. 'Am I missing something here?'

'I'm sorry, brother, I can't tell you yet,' said Lucius. 'Let's open it up and see if it's there first. Then you can read it and all will become clear.'

Quin's eyes narrowed. His friendly countenance became creased with suspicion. 'You *stole* the candelabrum!' he said. 'Hoping to find something incriminating, are you? I thought you'd given up trying to prove our uncle a villain.'

Lucius forced himself to ignore this. Agathon brought a knife and was soon working the blade into the crack of the tiny door, trying to lever it open.

It took a long time. While Agathon worked, Val entertained Quin with a few of Simio's tricks. Simmy was tired, and a little intimidated by Argos, but he was able to throw plums in the air and catch them in his hands, mouth or feet. Quin quickly recovered his good humour and laughed long and loud. Lucius couldn't enjoy the show, or even speak to Isi – usually the easiest thing in the world. He could only watch, his mouth dry with anticipation, as the tip of Agathon's knife worked away at the Menorah.

'Eureka!' Agathon eventually cried, as the little door popped open.

A heavy weight pressed on Lucius's chest. He could scarcely breathe. So much – *too* much – was hanging on the next few seconds. If there was nothing inside there, he thought he might simply collapse and die of disappointment.

'Can you see anything?' His voice emerged as a dry croak.

Agathon was frowning. He had his finger deep inside the stem, feeling around.

Then his face suddenly brightened, and it was as if the dawn had come early. 'Yes!' he cried. With excruciating slowness and care he began pulling out a parchment scroll. The letter had a broken seal. With shaking hands, Agathon examined the impression in the purple wax. 'It... it's the seal of Vespasian,' he said in a hollow voice. Then he sat up and stared at Lucius. 'By all the gods, boy – this has to be the letter your father referred to!'

With great reverence, he unfurled it and began to read aloud...

My dear Gaius Valerius Ravilla,

I write to express my gratitude for the brilliant work you have done over recent months in the service of the empire. The information you have provided was instrumental in the undoing of the Marcellus and Alienus conspiracy earlier this year and the Sidonius plot of last winter, as well as many other schemes against me and my family. Hundreds of traitors have now been executed, thanks to the vital intelligence contained within your letters. I sleep safer knowing that those who would conspire against me live in fear of the man they know only as the Spectre. Thank you, my friend.

Emperor Caesar Vespasianus Augustus

The words echoed in Lucius's ears like the notes of a cithara after it had ceased playing. He stared at the parchment scroll in Agathon's hands. It seemed extraordinary that this one short letter could contain so much power. The mere fact of its existence was enough to heal all the months of heartbreak. It would reunite him with his father, restore the family fortunes, and at the same time destroy his uncle, one of the most powerful men in Rome.

He felt Isi's hand close around his. He turned and saw her smile, and he realised he was crying. They hugged one another.

Quin was the first to speak. 'Give me that!' he shouted, snatching the letter from Agathon. Lucius observed the competing expressions in his brother's face as he took in the words written on the parchment. Disbelief turned to shock. Shock shaded into trembling anger. But within the anger, Lucius detected hints of shame, embarrassment and remorse.

The letter dropped to his lap as he stared at Lucius. 'I'm so sorry,' he said. 'Sorry I let myself be deceived by that... that *monster*, our uncle. Sorry I believed the accusations against Father. Sorry...' He couldn't continue. His hands rose to cover his face and his shoulders shook with sobs.

Agathon placed a comforting hand on Quin's arm. 'Do not be sad, Quintus,' he said. 'Your father will be able to return now. All his lands and titles will be restored to him. Your lives will be as before.'

'Not for me,' said Quin. His wet eyes stared bleakly ahead as if into a cold, dead future.

'Father will understand,' said Val. 'He will forgive –'

Quin gave an agonised roar. 'No! I don't expect or deserve his forgiveness. I betrayed him. I've been a fool!'

'You can make amends by helping us now,' said Lucius. 'We plan to take this letter to the Praetor's Office as soon it opens tomorrow morning. Will you come with us?'

'Of course!' said Quin, wiping his eyes. 'And I want to be there to witness Ravilla's face when he is arrested.'

'Do you mind if we stay here for the rest of the night, Agathon?' Lucius asked.

Agathon didn't answer, and Lucius noticed that the old man was now also crying. 'I'm sorry,' he eventually sniffed. 'I'm just so... so happy for you all. And for my dear old master Aquila.' He began sobbing again.

'You will come and live with us, Agathon,' said Lucius, recalling his earlier promise. 'And let us hear no more talk of *master*. You will live with us as our freedman tutor – and as our friend!'

Agathon smiled. 'That will be for Aquila to decide. Now, what were you saying just now? But of course you must all stay here. Though I'm afraid I can't offer you much comfort – or space!'

His guests found what floor space they could and tried to settle down to sleep. Lucius lay on the floor near the window, his hand resting lightly on Argos's soft shoulder. The night was warm and dry, and the moonlight streaming through the window turned the dog's dark fur a lustrous silver. In the shadows, he could make out Simio, the extraordinary chimp, curled up between Val and Isi. Quin yawned and stretched himself out near the door, and Agathon retired to his bedroom, taking the letter with him. Sleep seemed impossible. Lucius's mind reeled and shivered like a fresh-caught fish as he recalled what they'd achieved today and contemplated what they could look forward to tomorrow. Oh, but could they really stop Ravilla? Even now, that devious brain of his must be conjuring some means to thwart them.

Eventually, an hour or so before dawn, a nervous kind of sleep overtook Lucius. In his dreams he was running through the tunnels of the Hypogeum. It was hot and smoky from the burning torches. There were people chasing him. He could hear their footsteps echoing. They wanted the letter. He sensed them closing in. He could hear barking. They had dogs with them. He could feel hot, wet fur against his face. The tunnel was so smoky, he could scarcely breathe…

Lucius opened his eyes. The room was filled with thick, dark smoke. Argos was licking Lucius's face and whining – he'd been trying to wake him up. What was going on? Were those flames he could see coming from Agathon's bedroom? Val was bent over, coughing. Quin was on his feet, using his cloak to douse the flames, while Simio leapt about in a panic, screeching.

'We have to get out of here!' Isi shouted at him. 'The

building's on fire!' She helped Lucius to his feet and began pulling him towards the door.

'What about Agathon?' cried Lucius. Argos was howling and making desperate leaps towards the burning bedroom, but each time he was forced back by the intense heat.

'It's no use, I can't get in there!' cried Quin, helplessly waving his now flame-blackened cloak. 'If only we had some water!'

'I made a promise to him!' bellowed Lucius, tearing himself free of Isi's grip and plunging into the bedroom. The heat was indescribable – like having his skin ripped from his face. The smoke was like vitriol in his nose and throat, making him retch. He could see someone writhing in the flames – *Agathon!* – but couldn't reach him. Hands grasped him from behind and hauled him from the room. Numbly, Lucius saw that his tunic was on fire. Isi quickly smothered it with her cloak.

'Come on!' she cried. 'We have to save ourselves!' She led the way out of the apartment and down the stairs. Behind her followed Lucius and Val, with Simio in her arms, then Argos and Quin. The narrow stairwell was thick with choking smoke. Screams could be heard coming from other parts of the building. At last they burst into the street, collapsing to their knees and gulping air into their lungs. In the grey dawn light, they saw other refugees of the fire gathered there, wrapped in singed bedclothes, along with a crowd of gawpers from neighbouring insulae. Argos was racing around in circles, barking at everyone, then looking up towards the fourth-floor apartment window and whining pitifully.

'I'm sorry!' wept Val, sobbing into the dog's neck. 'He's gone, my darling. We just have to accept it.'

A bucket brigade soon formed – a chain of people stretching from the nearest fountain to the burning insula, passing buckets of water from person to person. But it was like trying to slaughter a bull with a hairpin. There were now smoke and flames pouring from every apartment window, and the wailing of those still trapped inside was horrible to hear.

'Send for the vigiles!'* demanded Quin hoarsely. 'We need men. We need pumps – or this will spread!' His face was so soot-blackened, no one recognised him as the Phoenix of Pompeii – though if anyone had, they would scarcely have been surprised to see him emerge alive from the conflagration. Nevertheless, they took up his cry.

'Send for the vigiles!'

But the vigiles did not come – at least, not to the Velabrum.

* *vigiles: the city watchmen, who were also the fire brigade.*

CHAPTER XI

1–6 JUNE

The warm, dry winds quickly blew the fire northwards. It swept through the Forum Holitorium – the vegetable market between the River Tiber and the Capitoline Hill – consuming everything in its path. As the sun rose into a sulphurous sky, the flames spread to the Campus Martius,* destroying houses, temples, theatres, sports arenas, market halls and government buildings. The inferno raged across the Campus Martius, and the vigiles did their best to contain it by using poles, hooks and even ballistae to tear down buildings in advance of the flames. They pumped water from the Tiber to attack

---

* *Campus Martius: the Field of Mars – an area outside the old city walls with many magnificent public buildings.*

the blaze and so managed to save several buildings that would otherwise have burned.

Many questioned why the vigiles had failed to attack the fire at its source in the Velabrum. Cynics assumed that the delapidated insulae of this impoverished neighbourhood were regarded by the authorities as more expendable than the wealthier mansions and public buildings of the Campus Martius. However, standing alongside Isi in one of the bucket brigades was a young fruit seller from the Forum Boarium. She'd been up early that morning, on her way to set up her market stall, when she saw a group of men gathered outside Agathon's insula. As she watched, they cast flaming torches into its lower windows, then ran away.

Isi rushed over to Lucius with this news. He was standing further along the same line, passing buckets. But he was doing so automatically – his mind seemed absent.

'Lucius!' she yelled.

He ignored her.

She grabbed him by the shoulders and shook him until he blinked and looked at her.

'Lucius, Agathon's building was set on fire by arsonists. It must have been Ravilla's doing. His men must have followed us here. *Ravilla* did this, Lucius! And then he must have bribed the vigiles so they wouldn't come.'

Lucius nodded, taking in this new information like a punch-drunk fighter absorbing yet another blow. His eyes were glazed with tears from smoke and sorrow, turning the world into a blurry vision of Hades. Inside he felt only a vast well of hopelessness. Agathon was gone. The letter was gone. What more was there left to fight for? Ravilla had won, as he always did and always would.

Later, they found Quin and Val helping burns victims onto an ambulance wagon. As the wagon moved off towards the hospital with its groaning cargo, Isi told them what she'd found out.

'He can't get away with this!' growled Quin.

'He has and he will,' said Lucius with cold finality.

'No!' cried Val. 'Don't give up on us, Lucius. This is the time we must be strong!'

'I'll denounce him,' Quin decided. 'As soon as the games restart, I'll denounce him in the arena – in front of everyone! Let him stand there before the people and deny it!'

'Shhh!' hissed Isi with a worried glance around her. 'If I know Ravilla, he'll have left a few spies on the scene, ready to listen in to our next move.'

Dejectedly, Lucius cast his eyes over the crowd. Everyone seemed innocent enough. But Isi was right: his uncle had ears and eyes everywhere. They could never defeat him, and the others were deluded for thinking otherwise.

Caecilia was both relieved and alarmed when Lucius and Valeria returned home later that morning. She had seen the huge pall of smoke rising over the other side of the city, and was shocked to see their singed and soot-blackened clothing. She also felt that the mysterious reappearance of Argos at their side merited some explanation. She had been out visiting with Gordianus and his friends the previous evening and hadn't seen the children go out; she had then spent the whole night worrying about what had become of them. Before her relief could turn to anger and a stream of questions, Val burst out with the tragic news of Agathon's death, before collapsing in sobs. Lucius, meanwhile, went and sat on the floor, entombed in his misery, absently stroking a still-whining Argos. Faced with this, Caecilia did the only thing she could think of, which was to prepare breakfast. Later, when the questions eventually started coming, Lucius was too depressed even to think of a decent lie, so Val came up with one instead. She said they'd been over at Agathon's last night because he'd been ill and needed looking after – she made no mention of Ravilla or the letter – and, fortunately, Caecilia seemed satisfied.

By the time the fire burned itself out three days later, many of the city's finest buildings lay in ruins, including Agrippa's Pantheon, the Temple of Jupiter, the Diribitorium, Pompey's Theatre and the Saepta Julia. It was the worst disaster to befall Rome since the Great Fire of sixteen years earlier, during the reign of Nero. Nero was so despised that some people claimed he had played his lyre while the city burned. But Titus was a different kind of emperor. Even while the fire was still raging, he was out in the streets offering words of comfort to the wounded. In the days that followed, he promised funds to rebuild and to compensate the residents for their losses. As for the games, they would continue as planned. As soon as he heard this news, Ramio came rushing into the quadrangle of the Morning School. 'The games are carrying on!' he cried.

Quin gave a whoop of joy and put down the weights he'd been exercising with. 'Did you hear that, Lu?' he said, turning to his brother, who was at that moment feeding his bears.

'I heard it,' said Lucius.

'So did I,' murmured Isidora. She was looking in on Kato in the next cage along. The tiger was prowling around his enclosure. His fur was glossy, his eyes sharp, and his paw – the formerly injured one – seemed to be giving him no trouble at all.

Lucius noticed Isi's worried frown. 'You were hoping the games would be cancelled, weren't you?' he said.

She nodded sadly. 'Hoping against hope for a reprieve for Kato.'

'He may not be called upon,' said Lucius.

'Are you kidding? Kato cost Silus a small fortune to procure. He isn't going to let these games pass without showing off his most prized specimen.'

Meanwhile, Ramio and Quin were discussing Quin's next outing in the arena.

'We're never going to be able to top what you did last time out,' said Ramio.

'And maybe we don't want to,' grimaced Quin, rubbing the still-sore wound to his shoulder.

'I was thinking that we ought to try something spectacular, though,' said Ramio. 'I mean, the games are drawing to a close, and it'll probably be your last fight. What about facing three animals? We could send out an elephant, a wolf and a leopard? I don't think we've done that combination before.'

'Leopards are horribly quick and unpredictable,' said Quin. 'To be honest, I'd rather face another lion.'

So engaged were they in this discussion that they failed to see the soldiers marching out of the building and heading swiftly towards them. But Lucius and Isi did see them, and started in alarm.

By the time Quin and Ramio looked up, six soldiers, armed with swords, stood before them.

'Quintus Felix?' said one of them, stepping forward and addressing Quin.

'It's Quintus *Valerius* Felix,' Quin corrected him – since learning the truth about his father, he'd decided to re-embrace the family name. He stood up and came closer to the soldier, squaring his shoulders as if preparing for a fight. 'What do you want with me?'

'Quintus Valerius Felix, by order of the emperor, you are hereby charged with starting the fire that began at Insula Flaminius on the Vicus Tuscus five nights ago. We are here to escort you to a prison cell to await your trial.'

'Now wait a minute!' cried Ramio. 'Quin would never –'

'Hush, Ramio,' said Quin calmly. 'This has to be Ravilla's doing. He must know I'm planning to expose him, and he wants to make the first move. But it's a ridiculous charge. Who could possibly believe that I had anything to do with starting that fire?'

Listening to all this, Lucius felt a tightening in his chest. He agreed with Quin that Ravilla had to be behind this, but didn't share his optimism that their uncle couldn't somehow make the charge stick.

'Take care, brother!' he cried, as the soldiers closed around Quin, seizing his arms and forcibly marching him away.

Quin looked back at Lucius and smiled. 'Don't worry, Lu. I'll explain everything to the magistrates. You just wait!'

Lucius didn't wait. Without even bothering to ask Silus for leave of absence, he headed straight over to the Praetor's Office to plead for Quin's release. The praetor and his staff occupied several rooms in the Basilica Porcia. Located on the northwest corner of the Forum, opposite the Senate House, the basilica was one of the grandest, most prestigious buildings in Rome.

The doorkeeper looked down his nose at the scruffy youth who showed up at his office in a shabby tunic smelling of animals. He was about to eject him from the building, until the boy explained that he was Lucius Valerius Aquila, nephew of Gaius Valerius Ravilla and brother of the great gladiator-turned-Bestiarius Quintus Felix, whose case he was here to plead. Lucius was soon ushered by a blue-liveried attendant down several long, echoing corridors, past innumerable marble busts of illustrious administrators from the city's past. He was told to wait in an antechamber, along with a dozen other petitioners, until such time as the praetor's assistant was free to see him.

It was deep into the afternoon by the time his name was called. He rose from the bench, stiff-limbed from waiting, and entered the office. The assistant was a middle-aged man with a round, fleshy face and fingers heavy with rings. He was attempting to swat a fly as Lucius came in. Eventually, he lifted his heavily lidded eyes and glanced up at Lucius with a bored expression. 'Yes?'

Undeterred by the man's look of bland indifference, Lucius launched into his plea.

'Yes, yes, I know all about this case,' the assistant swiftly interrupted. 'We have sworn statements from three independent eyewitnesses who all said they saw your brother starting the fire. I can show them to you if you like.' He began rifling through a pile of wax tablets on a table next to his desk, then shoved three of them in Lucius's direction.

Lucius flipped through the tablets. The witnesses' testimonies were hollow statements of fact, lacking any of the little details that might have marked them out as authentic.

'They're fake!' he declared, flinging them disdainfully onto the desk. 'Ravilla must have paid these people to say those things.'

The assistant raised his eyebrows at this. Lucius seemed finally to have captured his interest. 'I suppose you're referring to your uncle, the esteemed senator Gaius Valerius Ravilla. And why would he wish to pin the blame for the fire on your brother, his own nephew?'

'Because Quin was going to tell the world of his villainy, that's why! Ravilla started the fire. He tried to kill us, and destroy a letter in our possession from the Emperor Vespasian that proved that *he* was the Spectre, not my father!'

'Do you have any evidence to back up such a wild claim?'

Lucius stared at him forlornly. 'The evidence was the letter, which is now ashes.'

The assistant sighed. 'In that case, I'm afraid there's nothing I can do for you.' Noting Lucius's sullen expression, he added: 'I think it's safe to say this meeting is concluded.'

Lucius didn't move. 'When's the trial?' he asked.

The assistant consulted the water-clock behind him. 'The trial took place two hours ago,' he said.

'What?'

'Your brother was found guilty. He was sentenced to damnatio ad bestias, to be carried out at the Flavian Amphitheatre tomorrow morning.'

Damnatio ad bestias! Quin would be thrown into the arena to face the wild beasts without armour or weapons. It wasn't a fight, just a prolonged and very cruel form of execution.

Lucius learned that Quin was being held overnight in the prison at the Morning School. But when Lucius returned there, he was informed by the guards that his brother was not allowed visitors. So he went to Ramio for help. The beastmaster spoke to the school's head cook, and it was arranged that Lucius would take Quin his evening meal.

He found Quin alone in a cell not much bigger than a horse's stall, looking a far cry from the arena hero in gleaming armour. He was sitting hunched and unshaven on a pile of mouldering straw, a tick-ridden blanket covering his shoulders. The only thing they couldn't deprive him of was his smile, which lit up his face when he saw who was there.

Lucius handed him a bowl of cabbage, beans and vinegar water, and crouched down close to him so he could speak without being overheard by the guards outside. He wanted to say some words of comfort, but couldn't think of any.

'Fight of my life tomorrow,' Quin chuckled drily.

'I'm so sorry,' said Lucius.

'Listen,' murmured Quin. 'We did our best. Maybe if I hadn't been such a pigheaded fool for so long – if I'd realised a bit sooner that Ravilla was playing us along – I'd have been able to do something about it. By the time I came to my senses, it was too late.'

'Don't be too hard on yourself,' whispered Lucius. 'You did what you thought was right. That's all we can ever do… I just didn't expect the trial to be so quick. I thought we'd have some time to prepare a defence.'

'Our uncle has the praetor in his pocket, I've no doubt, along with most of the other city officials. We could never expect much in the way of justice. Did you see the names of those so-called eyewitnesses? Muco, Pansa, Lartius – they're all slaves from the Ludus Romanus – Ravilla's gladiator school! How convenient is that? I'll wager none of them were anywhere near Agathon's insula that night.'

'I could check them out,' Lucius offered. 'Maybe someone saw them at the school at the time of the fire.'

'Don't waste your time,' said Quin grimly. 'No one in that place would ever go against Ravilla.'

'Oy, you!' a guard called through the bars. 'You're supposed to be delivering food, not your life story. Now out of there!'

Quin grasped Lucius's arm. 'Farewell, Lucius!' he said, his voice thick with sadness and regret. 'Take care of Mother and Val for me. I'm sorry I couldn't do more, and that for so long I didn't believe…'

Lucius hugged him. He couldn't speak – his throat felt too tight.

'Keep up the fight for Father,' Quin whispered.

Isidora was waiting for Lucius at the gates of the Morning School. As he walked with her to her lodgings in the Ludus Romanus, he told her about his final conversation with Quin.

'I know Muco, Pansa and Lartius,' she said pensively. 'They're in the same accommodation block as me. I swear they were in their beds, along with everyone else, when I joined you that evening.'

'Yes, but you can't prove that they didn't get up early that morning and head over to the Velabrum.'

'Maybe I can,' she said. 'I can check the rosters – see who was on duty that morning.'

'Do what you can,' he said anxiously as they parted. 'We haven't much time.'

Back at home, he told Val and Caecilia the sad news about Quin. Val burst into tears. Caecilia, who had an impregnable faith in the city's justice system, merely nodded. 'If he's been found guilty, then he must be punished,' she said simply.

'Aren't you even sad, Mother?' sobbed Val.

'Of course I am,' answered Caecilia. 'And of course I shan't sleep tonight. But you cannot be the mother of a gladiator without mentally preparing yourself for something like this. Every time he steps into the arena, I expect him to die, while fervently hoping that he won't. The only difference this time is that his death is inevitable. There is no hope.' She looked at them, a slight frown creasing her smooth forehead. 'I do wonder, though, what possessed him to light that fire.' When her children didn't answer, she sighed and picked up her spindle. 'I expect that all this hero worship must have gone to his head. Perhaps he became unbalanced.'

CHAPTER XII

7 JUNE

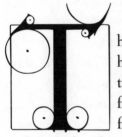he next morning at sexta hora, the hour before noon, every seat in the Flavian Amphitheatre was filled in anticipation of Quin's final appearance. It was the largest audience for the execution of a criminal that anyone could remember. As the great drum started to beat out its funereal rhythm, and Quin, escorted by six burly armed guards, appeared at the Gate of Life, a thunderous clamour filled the vast bowl. It was a chaotic mix of boos and cheers. The spectators appeared to be split into two camps – those who hated him for wreaking destruction on their city, and a smaller number of diehard supporters who'd probably love him whatever he did.

At his usual window in the room beneath the stands,

221

Lucius wiped a tear from his eye as he listened beneath the jeers and catcalls to the minority who were cheering. Quin's supporters were making a surprising amount of noise, and their defiance seemed to be infectious. As the boos gradually died away, the cheering continued, and the longer it went on, the louder it grew, until more than half the stadium seemed to be rooting for Quin.

This was extraordinary, considering that less than a week ago thousands of these people had lost loved ones, homes and possessions in the fire that Quin had been convicted of starting. Did this mean that they didn't believe the verdict, or was it just that they were prepared to forgive him anyway? Either way, it was a rousing, heartwarming send-off for Quin. Val, who had been inconsolable when Lucius left her this morning, would be comforted to learn that, at the very end, the ordinary people of Rome did not abandon their hero.

If only there were some way that these good people could be told the truth. Was a last-minute intervention possible? Lucius looked towards the emperor on his dais in the imperial box, surrounded by Praetorian Guards and the usual senior city officials. Might he grant a pardon? He would need firm evidence before going against the judgement of the praetor. Lucius hadn't seen Isi yet this morning, and had no idea if she'd managed to find out anything about those 'eyewitnesses' at the gladiator school. He didn't hold out much hope on that front. As Quin had said, no one in that place would want to defy Ravilla.

The crowd's cheers continued as the guards retired from the arena, leaving Quin standing alone in the centre, naked but for a loincloth. Titus did not seem particularly concerned by the tumultuous acclaim for a condemned criminal, though many of his officials looked unhappy about it. They were murmuring to each other and shifting uncomfortably in their seats. This was not in the script. Quin may have been a hero a week ago, but today he was most definitely a villain, and villains should not be cheered! Ravilla, seated near the emperor's right, was staring hard at Quin while whispering into the ear of someone next to him.

Lucius heard a flurry of complaints to his rear as someone fought their way through the crowd towards him. A breathless Isi finally surfaced nearby, clutching a pile of wax tablets.

'I've got them!' she cried.

'Got what?'

'Sworn witness statements from my old friends at the school. Look!' She handed him the tablets.

Lucius quickly read them:

I, Gemellus, head cook at the Ludus Romanus, swear that at prima hora on the Kalends* of June, Lartius the slave was on kitchen duty preparing breakfast.

* *Kalends: the first day of the month.*

Agorix, chief armourer at the Ludus Romanus, swears that Muco, his assistant, was helping him clean weapons in the armoury at prima hora on the Kalends of June.

I, Frontinus, assistant physician, do solemnly vow that on the Kalends of June at prima hora, Pansa was assisting me in the medical room at the Ludus Romanus.

Lucius stared at her excitedly. 'So they were all at the school, on duty, at sunrise – exactly when they were supposed to be at the Velabrum, according to their own witness statements!'

Isi nodded. 'Exactly!'

Hearing a low growl from the arena, they both turned to look out of the window. A large black bear had appeared on the sand. It was snapping angrily at its two heavily armoured handlers, who were goading it towards the centre of the arena with red-hot pokers. When the hungry beast arrived within scent of Quin it immediately forgot the handlers, who swiftly withdrew, and it began circling its new potential prey.

'Nemesis!' swore Lucius. 'I have to stop this!'

'Follow me!' said Isi, and she and Lucius ducked back into the crowd of slaves, which surged forward to take up the space they had vacated at the window. They battled their way across the room and through a door, then turned left and began racing up the tunnel that led to the Gate of Life and the arena. But before they could get there, they were intercepted by Silus, who emerged from a side tunnel.

'Ah! Isidora!' he grinned. 'Just the person I was looking for! I bring good news! I've discussed it with the Master of the Games and he's agreed that the tiger under your care should be one of the beasts used in this morning's damnatio.'

'No!' blurted Isi, before she could stop herself.

'What do you mean, *no*?' bristled Silus.

'I… I mean the tiger's not ready,' she stammered.

'Of course it's ready, you silly girl. I've just had it transferred from the Morning School, and it's now back in its old cage downstairs. Now come with me this instant and help the handlers move it into the elevator, or do you want a taste of my whip?'

As Silus began dragging her back down the side tunnel, Isi twisted herself back towards Lucius. 'Do what you can,' she mouthed before disappearing into the darkness.

Lucius stared at the tablets in his hands. It seemed so unlikely that he could do anything at this stage, but what choice did he have?

He ran down the remainder of the tunnel to the Gate of Life. Before the two guards on duty there could stop him, he barged between them and sprinted out into the sunlight and baking heat of the arena. A wave of nausea and dizziness overcame him as he took in the vastness of the crowd. The deafening volume of sixty thousand screaming voices made him want to fall to his knees and throw his arms over his head. Thirty paces ahead, he spied Quin doing his best to evade the hungry bear. As the bear advanced, Quin would back off or try to circle behind it.

Lucius heard shouts and running footsteps to his rear. The guards! He would have to act fast to get someone's attention. A few in the nearest seats had noticed him and were nudging their friends and pointing – but the ones he needed to speak to were in the imperial box. He sprinted towards the long northern curve of the oval arena, where the box was located, keeping well clear of the bear. He could hear the grunting breaths and heavy steps of the guards as they gained on him. Some of the crowd were laughing, assuming he'd been thrown on as comic relief, in case the execution wasn't engaging enough for them.

Twenty paces from the imperial box, Lucius halted and fell to his knees, holding aloft the tablets. 'Stop this!' he yelled. 'I have proof of his innocence!'

The officials were looking down at him curiously. He thought he might even have caught the emperor's eye, but he wasn't sure that anyone had heard him – the crowd's roar was so loud, it rolled and crashed around him like thunder. As he drew breath to try again, powerful hands clamped down on his arms and hoisted him to his feet. Other hands grabbed his ankles and he felt himself being carried backwards at great speed.

Still clasping the tablets tightly by his fingertips, he screamed 'I have proof!' towards the receding imperial box – but no one was listening. The guards carried him back through the Gate of Life and along the tunnel, with Lucius wrestling every step of the way to free himself. They were bundling him into a small, bare holding cell usually reserved for drunk or violent spectators, when a booming voice to the rear ordered: 'Halt!'

Lucius craned his neck to see who had spoken, and was relieved to see it was Ramio. 'Hand the boy over to me,' he said. 'He got a bit emotional just now. That's his brother out there. You have my word he won't disrupt this or any future event.'

'As you wish, Ramio,' said one of the guards. 'But you'll have the Master of the Games to answer to if he causes any more trouble.'

Lucius was dropped like a sack at the beastmaster's feet, and the guards returned to their station.

Ramio helped him up. 'By Juno,* Lucius. What were you trying to do out there? Do you think your mother wants to lose both her sons in one day?'

'Quin's innocent,' gabbled Lucius. 'I have proof. Ramio, you have to help me get word to the emperor before he's killed.'

'What are you talking about? What proof?'

Lucius showed him the tablets. 'These statements prove that the people who said they saw Quin starting the fire were nowhere near there at the time.'

---

* *Juno: the most important Roman goddess, wife of Jupiter and mother of Mars and Vulcan.*

Ramio shook his head. 'I don't know if you can call these things proof, my friend. It's just one person's word against another. But it may at least make them think again.'

'Will you help me get to the imperial box?'

'I can try,' he grunted. 'I only hope we're not too late. Your brother may already be bear food by now. Come on.'

Lucius raced after Ramio, out of the amphitheatre and into the crowded square. They ran around the base of the building, past the fast-food stalls and the betting stands, pushing their way through the press, until they came to the North Entrance, reserved for those of noble rank. Ramio showed his pass to the guard, explaining that Lucius was his guest, and they were waved through. They ran up a long, carpeted corridor with walls of fine plasterwork, decorated with paintings of gladiatorial combat.

'I won't be able to get us into the imperial box,' Ramio panted as they climbed a set of marble steps. 'I don't have that kind of clearance. But we can get into the senatorial seats just below, and maybe we can get a message passed along.'

They emerged into daylight. To either side of Lucius rose tier upon tier of terraced seating, with toga-clad aristocrats staring transfixed at the action in the arena.

Lucius hardly dared look at what was enthralling them. When he did, he saw that the bear had now been joined by a wild boar and, just entering through a trapdoor, was the enormous orange-and-black-striped man-killer that Isi affectionately knew as Kato. In between the three animals was Quin. He was lying on his side with a deep gash in his thigh.

This is the endgame, thought Lucius as the saliva in his mouth turned to sludge. The animals, all hungry, had scented Quin's blood. Instinctively they understood weakness in their prey, and they knew this could mean an easy meal to relieve the gnawing in their bellies. The bear was closing in. The boar was pawing the ground, preparing to charge. Kato was approaching stealthily, perhaps waiting for one of the other animals to make the first move before coming in to steal the prize.

'Come on!' boomed Ramio, shaking Lucius out of his momentary stupor.

They ran down some steps and along the parapet of the perimeter wall, drawing abusive complaints from the aristocratic spectators whose view they were momentarily blocking.

The imperial box loomed ahead. When they reached the base of its great, silk-shrouded dais, Ramio climbed some steps alongside it and spoke to a guard.

'We have an urgent message for the emperor!' he bellowed – but even Ramio's enormous voice was lost within the shrill howl that, just then, began swelling up around them. Terrified by the sound and what it might mean, Lucius spun around. He saw that Quin was back on his feet, staggering about, leaving bloody footprints in the sand from the gaping wound in his leg. He was trying to dodge the bear, which was towering over him and taking angry swipes at his head with its razor-sharp claws. But what had really energised the crowd was the wild boar, which now had its head down and was charging Quin from behind. Quin couldn't see this, and was probably too dazed to heed the warning shouts from the terraces. As the boar closed the gap, the bear made a wild sweep with its paw, which Quin also failed to see coming. It cracked him on the side of the head, sending him spinning into the sand. At that very instant, the boar struck – except that, with Quin down, it collided with the bear instead, goring it deeply in the belly with both tusks. In pain and confusion, the bear struck downwards with all its power, breaking the boar's neck. The two stricken beasts went down together in a death embrace. The bear roared and bit and scratched, while the boar squealed and gnawed and kicked, and soon their blood formed a shallow pool around them.

A few paces from this pair of flailing beasts lay Quin, face down and unmoving. The tiger approached the bear and boar and began licking at the blood. Then it latched its jaws onto one of the bear's arms and, with a casual flick of its great head, ripped the arm from its socket.

This was not what the organisers wanted to see. The beasts assigned to the damnatio should not be eating each other. The Master of the Games summoned the armoured animal handlers with their red-hot pokers, and soon the tiger, with the bear's arm still in its jaws, was being driven away from this easy feast. Slaves came on and stuck hooks in the corpses of the bear and boar, then dragged them through the Gate of Death to the spoliarium.

While all this was happening, Ramio and Lucius were doing everything they could to persuade the guard to let them into the imperial box, or at least pass on a message to the emperor. The guard, a fresh-faced youth only a few years older than Lucius, felt he lacked sufficient authority to agree to either of these requests, and instead went off to fetch his superior. Ramio and Lucius were forced to wait helplessly for the guard's return as the situation in the arena grew ever more deadly for Quin.

Kato, having devoured the flesh of the bear's arm in a few chomps, was staring hungrily at the fallen Bestiarius, who still lay unmoving on the sand.

Was he dead? Lucius thought he could discern faint signs of breathing, but he was too far away to be sure.

If sound alone could have roused Quin, then this crowd would certainly have succeeded in doing so. They shrieked and bellowed and roared at him for all they were worth. Yet still he did not move.

Having decided that Quin presented no threat, Kato gradually slunk closer and began sniffing at his lower leg. The tiger gave a feral roar that sent freezing nails into Lucius's blood. A slobber of saliva dripped from its mouth.

'Curses! Where is that guard?' glowered Ramio.

Lucius was too tense and frightened to reply.

With everyone watching and waiting so intently for the big cat to begin its feast, few noticed a nearby trapdoor open and a slender, olive-skinned girl step out into the arena. Dressed in nothing but a simple brown tunic, and carrying no weapon, she walked calmly up to the tiger.

As she drew closer, the murmurs of astonishment began.

'Isi!' murmured Lucius deliriously. He wondered if he was dreaming.

When it scented her, the tiger looked up from Quin and went slowly towards Isidora. To everyone's amazement, she held out her hand to the beast, palm up. The tiger opened its jaws wide, baring its teeth, and everyone assumed it was going to bite off her hand. Instead, it extended a long, pink tongue and licked her palm.

Shouts of 'Who is she?' and 'How can this be?' rose up from every part of the stadium.

Isi stroked Kato's head. She knelt down and embraced him, and many who saw this were certain they were witnessing a miracle.

Lucius sensed stirrings from above, in the imperial box. He looked aloft and saw that the emperor had risen from his throne.

Titus waited for the crowd to fall quiet. Then he spoke:

'When a young girl can walk up to a ferocious jungle beast and make it lick the palm of her hand, it is time for us to stop, listen and take note. It seems, to me at least, that the gods are determined that this man, Quintus Felix, shall live... And when the gods speak, who am I to defy their will?'

This speech was greeted with shocked silence. Titus sat down, and for a long moment no one seemed quite sure how to respond. Had the emperor just cancelled an execution because of a *girl*? Had such a thing ever happened in the whole history of the games? The air in the stadium seemed almost to split and crackle as if, with one sweep of his imperial hand, Titus had ripped out a page from the book of ancient tradition and burnt it before their eyes.

Then, down on the sand, something happened that completely changed the mood. Quin began to stir. After a moment, he sat up and looked around. As he did so, the uncertain silence was finally broken. Starting in the highest galleries, the shouts of thousands of voices began to fill the skies above the arena. Like a waterfall, their delight flowed rapidly downwards from tier to tier, gradually filling up the great bowl. Soon the stadium and the square beyond were rocking to the sounds of wild and riotous elation. For Lucius, the relief and ecstasy he felt at that moment was like a physical thing – as though he was being hugged simultaneously by everyone in the amphitheatre, as well as by all those cheering multitudes beyond. In reality, he found himself being swept up in a bearlike embrace from Ramio, which was so overpowering it almost felt like the same thing. Over Ramio's giant shoulder, he caught a glimpse of what was happening down in the arena: Isi, with Kato tamely in tow, was walking over to Quin and helping him to his feet.

Not everyone joined in the cheering. Large sections of the senatorial class remained stonily, disapprovingly silent, as did quite a number of the officials in the imperial box. As for Ravilla, Lucius noted with quiet satisfaction that he had become very flushed indeed, and his fists were squeezed tightly together as if he were hoping to find someone nearby to throttle.

CHAPTER XII

7–8 JUNE

Quin was taken to the medical room at the Morning School. As well as the wound to his thigh, he had suffered quite a severe head injury from the bear's sideswipe. Lucius and Isidora came with him and were there as Eumenes went to work on the injuries. Quin was dazed, but conscious.

Lucius held his hand. 'I believe you're going to be pardoned,' he told him.

'Then Ravilla will find some other way of finishing me off,' grunted Quin.

'Not in here – not while I'm around!' said Eumenes.

'And when Eumenes has to go out, Isi and I will be here,' added Lucius. 'You won't be left alone.'

'Isidora!' croaked Quin, twisting around to see her. 'Is it true what they say – that you saved me from the tiger?'

'I just directed his attention away from you,' she said. 'He knows me well.'

'She nursed him back to health,' explained Lucius.

Silus burst into the room, his face sweaty and pink with excitement. 'My girl! What a feat you just performed out there!' he said, striding up and kissing Isi on the cheek. 'I'll admit I was furious with you at first, but when I saw the reaction of the emperor – and the crowd! Why, that tiger is a star! I always said it was worth keeping it alive, did I not? And now I have such plans for it.' He rubbed his hands in gleeful anticipation. 'We're going to send it out against a rhinoceros next, and then two bulls. And maybe eventually a rematch with the great Phoenix of Pompeii himself!' He grinned toothily at Quin. 'This time you would have weapons, of course…'

Isi's face fell. 'I… I think Kato's famous for granting *life*,' she said hesitantly, 'not for dealing death.'

Silus's flush darkened to anger. 'What are you…?'

The rest of this question was lost beneath the piercing sound of trumpets. The door to the medical room was flung wide and a dozen soldiers of the Praetorian Guard marched in.

Oh no! thought Lucius. *Ravilla has sent these men to finish us off!*

The soldiers, intimidating in their gleaming silver

helmets and breastplates and their crimson cloaks, positioned themselves at the door and the windows, preventing any possibility of escape or rescue for those in the room.

Ravilla then entered, and with him – to everyone's shock and amazement – was the emperor. Titus, swathed in imperial purple and gold trim, was short in stature. His famously square jaw had, in recent years, rounded and fattened into a double chin, and his skin was as peach-soft and smooth as an infant's. Yet the man had an extraordinarily commanding presence, and Lucius was reminded that he had been a successful military general long before he became emperor. He felt another brief moment of dizziness, like the one he'd felt on rushing into the arena, as he took in the fact that he was now standing just a few short paces from the man whose image appeared on pedestals, coins and frescoes from Caledonia to Numidia.*

Ravilla, alongside him, was smiling with his mouth, but his eyes were dark with the frustrated anger of a wolf beaten to its feast by a lion – this impromptu imperial visit had clearly not been his idea. Other officials and more guards flowed in behind them before the door was finally closed.

Silus ballooned with pride when he saw the emperor, clearly assuming he was about to be personally congratulated. 'Imperial majesty, I am most deeply

---

* *Caledonia: Scotland; Numidia: a Roman province in North Africa, in present-day Algeria and Tunisia.*

honoured by this visit,' he fawned, sinking to his knees and abasing himself before Titus. 'All the many hours of painstaking work that I put into that performance by my tiger this morning, I most humbly dedicate to you and to the memory of your divine father.'

Titus eyed him with a mixture of amusement and distaste. 'What is your name?' he asked.

'Silus, my lord.'

'I didn't see *you* out there today, Silus. I saw… *her.*' He flung a pudgy, beringed finger towards Isi.

Silus laughed nervously. 'Of course, Divinity, it would not have been *I* who actually, er…'

'And pray explain to me, Silus, what exactly you were doing training a tiger assigned to the damnatio to lick a girl's hand? Perhaps at the next execution, you'll get the bear to do a little dance, hm?'

Some of the officials behind him laughed.

'I, er…' Silus's voice trailed off uncertainly. He seemed to have dwindled in size somehow as he slunk, embarrassed, to a corner of the room.

'Fear not, Silus,' said the emperor dismissively, 'it was not you who were behind this morning's performance, but the gods. Through the agency of the girl and her tiger they have declared that a condemned man shall live.' He examined Quin as he lay there being treated by Eumenes. Quin had lapsed into a semi-stupor, his eyes barely open. Yet the emperor did not seem to realise this as he went on. 'The deities appear to have forgiven you, Quintus Felix,' said Titus gravely, 'and

I am sorely tempted to do likewise. Indeed, as I recall your celebrated feats in the arena, it seems to me that the only fire you are guilty of starting in this city is the one you have lit in the hearts of its people. However, just as I cannot ignore the verdict of the gods, I feel unable to disregard the decisions of my magistrates. I have therefore decided to commute your sentence to exile.'

Hearing this, Lucius knew he had to intervene. Calling up all his courage, he stepped forward. 'Caesar, may I speak?'

Titus eyed him curiously. 'Are you not the crazed boy who ran into the arena this morning? I was informed that you are the brother of Quintus.'

'I am, sire.'

'What do you wish to say to me?'

'That th-there... there...' The words, which he'd waited so long for a chance to say, stuck fast on his tongue. He was acutely aware of Ravilla's eyes on him, his lips twisted into a wolfish sneer. *Snivelling wretch,* he seemed to be saying, *you wouldn't dare, would you? You haven't the mettle to go up against me...*

Titus was growing impatient. 'What is it, boy? Speak!'

A vision came to Lucius then of Agathon writhing in the flames. Anger swelled within him, unblocking his tongue. 'My brother did not start that fire,' he said. 'The eyewitnesses who said they saw him were never there at the time. I have evidence, Caesar.' He held up the tablets.

'Show me those,' commanded Titus.

Shaking, Lucius handed them to the emperor.

Titus perused them carefully before handing them to one of his advisors. 'These statements,' he said, 'do seem to call into question the veracity of the witness accounts which, I think I'm right in saying, were a key element in the case for the prosecution.'

'Indeed they were, Caesar,' said the advisor.

'In that case, we must recall the original witnesses, together with the authors of these latest statements, and see if we can find out the truth.'

The advisor bowed. 'I will see to it at once.'

As he started towards the door, Ravilla spoke up: 'Caesar, the witnesses are all slaves working at my gladiator school. With your permission, I would be happy to question these individuals myself.'

Titus frowned. 'Gaius, as the uncle of the defendant, I'm not sure it would be wise for you to get involved.'

'I understand, Caesar,' said Ravilla, bowing his head. 'However, I know these fellows, and I believe I would be best placed to discover the truth. Of course, I vow to act with strict impartiality.'

'Very well,' said Titus.

'He'll kill them!' screamed Lucius. The words were out before he could stop them.

Every eye in the room swung back towards him, including the emperor's. Titus's glare was like a steel blade held before his face. 'Explain yourself, boy!' he said icily.

Lucius knew his cheeks were burning and his hands were shaking, but he didn't care. Now that his moment had finally arrived, he felt a thrilling kind of energy coursing through him. 'My uncle will kill them before they can confess,' he spluttered.

'And why would he do that?' demanded Titus.

'Because he wouldn't want the truth to come out that he paid them to give false testimony.'

Surprised murmurs washed around the room. Titus turned in bewilderment to Ravilla. 'What *is* this boy talking about, Gaius?'

'I have no idea, sire,' said Ravilla, a small smile edging its way onto his face.

In his fury, Lucius almost forgot who he was addressing. He began waving his arms about as he cried: 'My uncle wanted Quin dead, because Quin was going to tell the people about the letter!'

Titus was starting to look exasperated. 'What letter?'

'The letter from your father, sire, which confirmed that Ravilla was the Spectre!'

The murmurs turned into cries of outrage. There were yells of 'Monstrous!' and 'How dare he?' from the toga-clad officials. Lucius was sure that he was about to be arrested. However, the emperor seemed to take his accusation quite calmly – and so, disturbingly, did Ravilla.

'Show me this letter,' ordered Titus.

'I wish I could,' said Lucius. 'Unfortunately, it was destroyed in the fire.'

241

Titus closed his eyes briefly and nodded to himself. 'Yes, that *is* unfortunate – for *you*!' He turned to Ravilla. 'What do you have to say about all this, Gaius? *Were* you the Spectre?'

Ravilla's upper lip curled with mirth. 'I cannot claim that honour.'

'Yes, I rather thought you might say that!' chuckled Titus. 'Do you know anything about this letter?'

'No, I do not.' Ravilla's amusement had vanished. He turned to Lucius with an expression of sad puzzlement. 'And I cannot understand why Lucius would think such things of me. I can only imagine that the revelations concerning his father last year have caused him to lose his wits. It breaks my heart to hear these allegations from my own nephew after all I have done for him and his family over the past eleven months.'

'He's lying,' cried Lucius desperately, feeling the battle slipping away from him. 'We saw the letter with our own eyes. We –'

'Silence!' snapped Titus, his voice as hard and sharp as a hurled spear. 'I've heard enough from you today, young man. If you learn anything from this experience, remember never to make allegations against people unless you have the evidence to back them up. Now, let us leave this place!'

With a sweep of purple and gold, the emperor turned around and began making swiftly for the door, as advisors, officials and guards hastened to keep pace.

Lucius felt a crushing sensation in his chest – the death of hope.

Then, from near the back of the emperor's retinue, a high-pitched voice trilled: 'Caesar!'

Titus stopped, but remained facing the exit. 'Yes, Casca,' he said wearily, for he must have recognised the voice.

An elderly man stepped clear of the crowd of advisors. 'Caesar, it may interest you to know that your father kept copies of all his correspondence.'

Hearing this, Titus finally turned.

Lucius's skin prickled as he saw a flash of alarm pass through Ravilla's eyes.

'It was at the insistence of his late mistress, Caenis,' continued Casca. 'She was worried that people might try to misrepresent the emperor, so –'

'Where are the copies held?' interjected Titus.

'In the library rooms off the east courtyard of the Old Palace,' answered Casca.

'Then you must organise a search for this letter,' said Titus, casting an eye back towards Lucius. 'And we'll see if the boy spoke the truth.'

Ravilla gave a start of surprise on hearing this instruction, but said nothing.

The following evening, Lucius received a summons to the Palace of the Caesars. For the second time in three months, a grand litter, borne by liveried attendants, appeared outside his humble Suburran insula. Valeria was there to see him off. His mother remained in the apartment in a mild state of shock.

The previous evening, Lucius and Val had decided to come clean with her about all they'd been up to over the past three months. She'd reacted with cold-eyed fury upon learning how they'd risked their lives and incurred the wrath of their protector for what was, to her, clearly a mistaken and futile cause. In her rage, she'd threatened all sorts of things, from disowning them to killing herself. 'This will end in disaster,' she predicted with all the sage certainty of an augur* studying the flight of ravens.

So when the summons to the palace came earlier that day, presenting the possibility that Lucius and Val might have been right all along, Caecilia didn't know how to react. She watched, trance-like, from her window, her mouth agape at the opulence of the litter and its bearers.

'Good luck, Lu,' smiled Val before he climbed aboard. She kissed him on the cheek. 'I expect you to tell me everything when you get back – every little detail, from the colour of the curtains to what you had for dinner – OK? Take notes if you have to.'

The litter attracted stares from the customers queuing up at Calva's Thermopolium, and this time

---

* *augur: a priest who was believed to be able to interpret the will of the gods by observing natural phenomena.*

Calva had his story prepared. 'Oh yes,' he said grandly, waving at Lucius and Valeria. 'Those are my good friends from the upstairs flat – they're from a patrician family, don't you know? Fallen on hard times recently, but they still dine regularly with their rich friends up on the hill – though they always tell me the grub they get served on the Palatine isn't a patch on mine!'

As Lucius progressed smoothly through the streets in his covered chair, he tried to calm his heart. *This has to be good news, right?* he reassured himself. *They must have found a copy of the letter. Otherwise, why would they bother summoning me to the palace?* Yet every time these optimistic feelings surged into his mind, he batted them away. So often over the past eleven months his hopes had risen, only to be brutally dashed. Why should this occasion be any different? Maybe the letter *hadn't* been found, and they were calling him in to punish him for slandering a senior imperial official. Or maybe this was all some elaborate and sadistic trick of Ravilla's, and he would find himself not in the emperor's palace but in a cold, dark cell where he'd be tortured, then murdered.

He glanced nervously between the curtains of the litter as they ascended the Palatine Hill, and was relieved when they passed beyond Ravilla's house and began approaching the palace environs. As they neared its gates, they encountered a crowd of petitioners and idle bystanders. Way-clearers used their whips to beat a path through the throng. The palace rose up before him – tier on tier of pale colonnades, lit by hundreds of crystal lamps. He was carried into a vast hall, with a domed ceiling as high as the clouds, supported by enormous columns of red granite. He stared at the polished walls of crimson-veined marble lined with exquisitely smooth alabaster statues, and fountains alive with nymphs* spouting water into iridescent pools.

The litter was set down and Lucius was led across the room by white-liveried servants. He felt as though he was floating rather than walking, lulled by the beauty, the sweet, spicy scents, and the silky music that played over the sound of rushing water. Vague concerns wafted through his brain: *I don't belong here... My place is in the stinking caverns beneath the amphitheatre... There's been a mistake... Oh, how will I be able to describe all this to Val?*

He was led towards the emperor, who was seated on a tall, narrow throne, raised up on a dais, and wore a heavy, gem-studded diadem on his head. Titus was surrounded by beautifully dressed courtiers, both men and women. There was so much to take in, but Lucius tried to memorise at least a few details. *His throne has lion-headed, ivory armrests. The women of the court are swathed in crimson. Their hair flashes with precious stones.* He was horribly conscious of his own humble tunic of rough, undyed wool.

---

* nymphs: nature spirits in the form of beautiful young women.

Just then his roving eye spotted Ravilla, standing a little way to his left, also facing the throne. His uncle looked anxious, he was pleased to note, with dark patches under his eyes indicating lack of sleep. It would seem that for Ravilla, also, this summons had been unexpected.

'Welcome, Lucius,' beamed Titus when he saw him. 'Thank you for coming. You'll be pleased to hear that our search of the archives in the Old Palace has borne fruit. We have found the letter you spoke of!'

As the emperor said this, his gaze switched to Ravilla, who jerked as if prodded sharply by someone to his rear. His eyes grew very wide and his jaw trembled.

'Caesar,' stammered Ravilla, 'I... I'm sure you have not forgotten how Caenis was despised by everyone while she was alive – you made no secret of your own animosity towards her. She wielded a most deplorable influence over your father in his declining years. Are you really going to place your trust in anything found in an archive over which she presided?'

Titus smiled. 'You're right, Gaius. I didn't care much for the woman. But I never doubted that she loved my father and would do anything in her power to protect him. She was proud, power-hungry and paranoid, but she was always scrupulously honest. I only wish the same could be said for the informers in the network she helped to create.' He scrutinised Ravilla as he said this, and his steely eyes appeared to soften with regret.

Lucius watched his uncle's face twist into something almost bestial. His nostrils flared and his thin lips spread into a bare-toothed snarl as he cried: 'But she hated me! She wanted to destroy me, and I see the evil witch can still exercise her perverted influence from beyond the grave. I thought you were a better man than your father, Titus! But she has you just as spellbound by her vicious lies!'

'Watch your tongue, Gaius!' growled the emperor. 'Remember who you're addressing! Anyway, her feelings towards you are immaterial. The seal on the letter was unbroken when it was discovered in the library this morning. It has been checked by experts and they have all confirmed that it is in my father's hand. There is no longer any point in denying that you were the Spectre. It is also a matter of record that you were instrumental in the witch-hunt against your brother Aquila, forcing him into exile. My spies have been keeping tabs on Aquila, as they do on all exiles, and it may disappoint you to know that he has been living in reasonable contentment as an olive grower in Perugia. As we speak, a messenger is on his way there to inform him that all charges against him have been dropped and he is free to return to Rome. As for you, my old friend, I'm afraid the future does not look quite so rosy.'

Listening to these words, Lucius felt himself melting with pure joy. If clouds had parted just then and Mercury, the messenger of the gods, had welcomed him to the Fields of Elysium,* he could not have felt happier. He had a vision of his father, labouring in the olive groves, being approached by a white-liveried messenger with a scroll.

Ravilla, meanwhile, seemed to be undergoing some sort of inner collapse. His chest began to heave at an unnatural rate. His cheeks had darkened and a violent twitch had started up just below his right eye. Titus nodded to some guards who had been quietly moving themselves into position just behind him. Two of them now stepped forward and grabbed Ravilla by the arms, while another manacled his hands behind his back.

As he was led away, Ravilla twisted his head and yelled: 'Titus, I've always been your most loyal servant and friend! Let me speak, I beg you! You owe me that much, Titus! Let me explain myself!'

'You'll get your chance in court,' replied Titus. 'Unlike your victims, I intend to give you a fair trial.'

---

* *Fields of Elysium: the place where the blessed were thought to go after death.*

EPILOGUE

11–18 JUNE

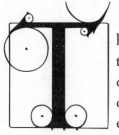hree days later, Aquila returned to Rome. He rode in a four-horse carriage specially provided by courtesy of the emperor, and he entered the city through the narrow gate to the north known as the Porta Salaria. In his hand he carried a letter from Titus offering him a formal pardon and the immediate restoration of all his titles and estates. An old senatorial friend, currently residing on his country estate, had offered Aquila and his family temporary residence in his mansion on the Esquiline Hill, until such time as their original house could be repurchased from the people it had been sold to.

Aquila's carriage was met in the Forum by an

imperial honour guard. Also present to greet him were Caecilia, Lucius, Argos, Valeria and a limping, bandaged Quintus. Aquila looked leaner than Lucius remembered, but he also glowed with the kind of vitality that only outdoor, country life can bring.

When it was Lucius's turn to receive his father's greeting, he could not help the tears falling. Aquila's strong hands closed around his shoulders, and his warm, intelligent eyes looked deeply into his son's. In that one searching look, his father seemed to understand and appreciate all Lucius had been through.

Caecilia seemed awkward with her husband. She embraced him dutifully, but Lucius sensed a stiff formality between them that hadn't been there before. He hoped that, in time, some sort of reconciliation might be possible. But deep down he knew that her lack of faith in her husband at the time when he needed it most had fractured something deep in their relationship and it would never be the same again.

Unlike Caecilia, Valeria radiated pure happiness and love for her father. Forgetting that they were surrounded by soldiers in ceremonial uniform, she hugged him with fierce abandon, and then would not stop chatting about all the things that had happened to them over the past year. When she could no longer think of things to say, she began plying him with questions, which, together with Aquila's answers, took up most of the journey to the palace, where Aquila was formally welcomed back by the emperor.

That evening, as the family sat around the fire, Lucius showed his father the flame-charred Menorah, which he'd managed to retrieve the day before from the ruins of Agathon's insula. Aquila appraised the candelabrum with a frown. 'What an object to use to hide a letter!' he exclaimed. 'My brother clearly had no sense of its significance as a sacred relic. We must make sure it goes back to the Jewish community in Judea. I will organise its return.'

'Father,' said Valeria in an unusually shy voice, 'speaking of the Menorah, you remember how we got hold of it originally, don't you? How Simio managed to...? Well, I was sort of thinking how much we owe him, and how he's still living in a crate in that courtyard in Suburra, and...' She trailed off.

Aquila smiled. 'I don't think it would be out of the question to build some sort of animal enclosure in the garden of our house, once we get it back. What do you think, Valeria?'

A shiver of excitement went through her. She clasped her hands. 'Oh, Father, can we?'

'Of course, your mother would have to agree,' continued Aquila. 'But I can't see that she would object to something small – a pleasant home for, say, a very clever and heroic chimpanzee.'

'Oh, yes!' cried Val. 'Can we, Mother? Can we?'

Caecilia shrugged. 'So long as it doesn't come into my part of the house, I have no objection.'

The following day brought grim news. Ravilla, who was being held in the Tullianum prison beneath the Forum, had decided not to wait for his trial. A loyal servant from the gladiator school had bribed one of the guards to look the other way while he sneaked a knife into his master's cell. Ravilla's body had been found in the morning.

Lucius reflected on his feelings about this, but could not bring himself to feel much pity for a man who had destroyed the lives of so many. Aquila, as Ravilla's closest living relative, inherited his estate – some compensation, perhaps, for the pain his brother had caused him and his family. Among the property of that estate was a certain slave called Isidora. At Lucius's request, Aquila manumitted her.

'What will you do now?' Lucius asked Isi now that she was free.

The question made her smile. 'No one's ever asked me that before,' she said. 'It's always, "Isidora, do this… Isidora, do that!" Ask me it again, Lucius.'

He did so.

She gave the question a lot of deep thought.

Lucius started to wonder if all this deliberation was just politeness or shyness on her part – though he'd never have thought to attribute the latter quality to Isi. Eventually, he said: 'You can come and live with us, if you want, Isi – I mean as a member of the family.'

'Oh, Lucius,' she cried. 'I'd so love that, you know I would, but…'

'But?'

'But I think I really ought to go home.'

'Home? What home?'

'Egypt.'

'But, Isi, you've never been to Egypt in your life. Your parents were taken from there before you were born.'

'I know, but I feel it's where I belong. I want to do this for my parents, and for me. The Romans ruptured my family's story by taking my parents away from their homeland, and I want to heal the breach by returning. I want to marry an Egyptian man and have Egyptian children, and tell them about their grandparents, how they were stolen away, and how I, their daughter, returned. I don't expect you to understand, I just know it's what I must do.'

'I'll miss you,' said Lucius.

'I'll miss you, too.' She hugged him, and he heard her sniff away a tear. 'But we'll always have the memories of our adventures. That will link us, however far apart we are.' She wiped her eyes. 'By the way, Lucius, if there's room in your new animal enclosure, I have a rather amazing tiger that's looking for a home.'

'I'll see to it,' he whispered hoarsely.

More days passed and, for the family of the Valerii, life began to settle into a quieter rhythm. But Lucius could tell his brother was not quite happy inside. He had something he needed to say to his father. One afternoon, Aquila, Lucius and Quin were sitting on a bench by a fountain in the garden. Argos was there, too, watching the fish in the pond. Lucius was listening to his father reading a passage from Pliny's *Natural History* when Quin suddenly interrupted.

'Father,' he said. 'You should know that Lucius and Valeria never once lost faith in you. I wish I could say the same for myself.'

Aquila put down the book when he heard this and placed a reassuring hand on his elder son's shoulder. 'Quintus, your great strength is that you always see things exactly as they appear, and then act accordingly. You're as bold and straightforward as a lion, and that's what made you such a great fighter. Don't blame yourself for behaving according to your nature – I certainly don't. I never once stopped loving you throughout all my time away. I've always known that you have a good soul, Quintus, and you proved it at the end. Because when you were presented with evidence of my innocence, you unhesitatingly embraced the truth.'

It seemed as though a weight had fallen from Quin's shoulders when he heard Aquila say this. 'The truth,' he murmured to himself. 'The truth is, Father, I never stopped loving you, either.'

Aquila smiled at this. 'Speaking of fighting,' he said, 'are you still determined to pursue a career in the arena?'

Quin shook his head. 'No, Father, my fighting days are definitely over. I've done with killing men and beasts.' Then a gleam came into his eye and he rose to his feet. He stood, legs akimbo, and mimed holding a rein and a whip. 'My destiny,' he announced, 'is the Circus Maximus. I'm going to be the finest chariot racer the world has ever seen!'

END OF BOOK 3

AUTHOR'S NOTE

In writing this book, I have drawn from many sources to try to create a realistic picture of life in Rome in AD 80. Although the story is fictional, I have woven in real historical events from that year, including the Inaugural Games of the Flavian Amphitheatre (better known today as the Colosseum) and the fire that devastated the northwest quarter of Rome. For the purposes of my plot, the fire began in a district called the Velabrum – in fact, no one knows where or how it started. I have also made reference to some real historical events that occurred in the years prior to AD 80, including the Great Fire of Rome (64), the destruction of the Temple of Jerusalem (70) and Agricola's conquest of the Ordovices tribe in present-day Wales (76). Carpophorus, whom I briefly mention as a famous Bestiarius, was a real-life star of the Inaugural Games. The scene in which the fierce tiger Kato licks Isidora's hand in the arena was inspired by an actual event that apparently occurred at those games; the Roman poet Martial described the incident as 'unknown in any age'.

FOLLOW LUCIUS'S FURTHER ADVENTURES IN:

GLADIATOR SCHOOL 4
BLOOD
VENGEANCE

It was the eighth day of the Ludi Romani – the Roman Games. Marcus Acilius Glabrio, Consul of Rome and sponsor of the games, dropped his white cloth, signalling the start of the race. The twelve starting gates sprang open and out charged the charioteers. The air exploded with the exhilarated cries of 150,000 spectators, as hoofbeats echoed like thunder around the vast, elongated bowl of the Circus Maximus.

Lucius, seated in the stands next to his father, Aquila, strained to identify his brother Quintus among the racers, but all he could see at first was horses and clouds of dust. The bright sunlight forced him to squint. Then the charioteers came into view, biceps gleaming as they gripped the reins and lashed their horses, urging them faster. The drivers, hunched in their flimsy wooden chariots, were dressed in simple tunics in their team colours – red, white, blue and green. Each team was running three chariots today, and each chariot was pulled by a team of four horses, making for a crowded track. Lucius, who had never previously been the slightest bit interested in chariot racing, was now a firm fan of the Whites, but only because it was Quin's team.

'There he is!' he cried, suddenly spotting Quin's dusty white tunic and the golden-blond curls poking out from beneath his helmet. 'He's second, I think – or maybe third.' There were so many chariots all bunched together, it was hard to be sure.

Lucius and Aquila were in the senatorial seats to the right of the imperial box, on the opposite side of the stadium to the starting gates. They momentarily lost sight of the chariots as they passed behind a towering red granite obelisk, located halfway along the spina – the strip that ran down the centre of the long, oval track. When Quin appeared again, his chariot was hemmed in among a cluster of others, close to the high stone wall of the spina.

'Why are they crowding him like that?' Lucius shouted, alarmed.

'I have no idea,' replied Aquila, who greatly preferred the scholarly silence of the library to the frenzy of the race track and looked thoroughly out of place. 'But it may interest you to know that that giant obelisk was brought to Rome from Egypt by the emperor Caligula.'

Lucius barely heard him. 'They're going to crash if they're not careful!' he shouted.

Aquila's friend and fellow senator, Galerius Horatius Canio, leaned across Aquila to make himself heard to Lucius. 'They're all trying to position themselves close to the spina,' he explained. 'It's the best place to be. Your brother must hold his nerve, and his position, and not be crowded out. But watch out for the turns – that's where most of the crashes happen.'

Lucius watched, gripped by the drama, as four of the chariots – Quin's included – vied for pole position closest to the spina. The horses' muzzles were flecked with foam and their eyes bulged frantically while each driver fought to inch ahead of his rivals. By the time they reached the turning post at the end of the spina, Quin was narrowly in the lead.

'He's done it! He's in front!'

'It's a long race,' cautioned Canio.

Lucius stared, heart in mouth, as his brother pulled his horses into a tight turn at high speed, only just avoiding a collision with the turning post. Meanwhile, a desperate tussle for third place between a Green and a Red charioteer led to the first accident of the afternoon. Green must have pushed Red too tightly against the turning post, for suddenly Red's chariot flipped onto its side. The Red driver tumbled out and was then pulled along the track by his panicked horses.

'Why doesn't he let go of the reins?' cried Lucius.

'He can't,' responded Senator Canio. 'He's wrapped them around his waist – the riders do that so they can use their body weight to control the horses. Now he must use his knife to free himself.'

Lucius watched open-mouthed as the rider was hauled painfully along the dusty track. But before he could cut himself free of the reins, he disappeared under the hooves of a team of horses coming up behind. Lucius caught a horrific glimpse of the rider being crushed beneath the horses' hooves and the wheels of the chariot. The Red driver's mangled, bleeding body lay there on the sand until stretcher-bearers were able to dash onto the track and carry it away.

The other charioteers safely negotiated the turn and began racing once more along the straight. Quin had managed to maintain his position on the innermost part of the track, but was facing severe competition from a Blue charioteer, who was now neck-and-neck with him. The rivals urged their horses faster with cracks of their whips. They seemed entirely equal in speed and strength. On the second turn, Blue made his move: he turned more tightly than expected, straying into Quin's line and forcing Quin even closer to the turning post in order to avoid a collision. There was an audible crack as Quin's axle hit the post's semicircular base. His chariot wobbled, and for a second Lucius was sure he would be upended and would share the gruesome fate of the Red charioteer. But somehow, Quin managed to keep his chariot balanced, and on they went. The wobble must have slowed or unnerved him, though, because Blue now edged in front.

The other charioteers soon followed around the turn. A bell sounded and one of the seven bronze dolphins suspended above the turning post lowered its head, marking the completion of the first lap. The race settled into a steadier pattern on the second lap, with Blue in the lead, Quin in second place, Green in third and the rest strung out behind. Green was gaining on Quin, though, and it didn't take Lucius long to figure out why: as Quin passed beneath Lucius's seat for the second time, he noticed that his brother's chariot wheel – on the side where the axle had grazed the turning post – was wobbling very slightly, and this was slowing him down. Yet Quin was stubbornly resisting Green's attacks, skilfully cutting him off every time he tried to edge past on the inside.

'Quintus is displaying admirable perseverance and skill,' commented Canio, who was a seasoned racegoer, 'but I fear he won't be able to hold off the challenge from Bassus for long.'

The battle for second place between Quin and Bassus of the Greens was obsessing everyone, to judge from the noise levels. The stadium had become a billowing sea of green and white banners as supporters of the rival teams tried to out-shout each other.

Shortly after the fourth bronze dolphin had lowered

its head, there was another crash, and this time it was a big one. A member of the Greens, under pressure from a White, lost control and smashed his chariot against the spina. The pursuing White was unable to swerve in time and ploughed straight into the upended chariot, killing the Green charioteer. Then a Blue, just behind him, crashed into the wreckage. This caused a domino effect, and in the blink of an eye five chariots had crashed out of the race. The accident happened right under Lucius's nose, so he was forced to witness, in sickening close-up, the deaths of five charioteers, and perhaps twice that number of horses. The track beneath him looked like a battlefield, strewn with blood-soaked men and twitching, frightened horses alongside the splintered remains of chariots.

The slaves who were employed to keep the track clear during races now had the dangerous task of removing the bodies and the wreckage, while the race continued around them. A couple of slaves were a little too slow at evading oncoming chariots, and they, too, lost their lives.

When Quin swerved to avoid the wreckage, Bassus seized the opportunity to overtake, pushing Quin into third place. And, with his damaged wheel, it seemed he had little chance now of improving on this position.

'It looks as though your brother may have to settle for third,' said Canio. 'Still, not too bad for a boy who's only been racing for a year.'

Once he was past Quin, Bassus rapidly closed in

on his next target, the Blue charioteer who had been leading the field since the second lap. As the final lap commenced, the two became locked in a tight contest, while behind them Quin came under pressure from the fourth-placed Red charioteer, who was steadily overtaking him on the outside.

So, the crowd's attention became split between two battles: between Blue and Green for first place, and between White and Red for third. Fights broke out between rival fans, as excitement spiralled into hysteria. Then Blue and Green turned into the final straight and two things happened that changed the race completely...

TO BE CONTINUED...

FIGHTERS IN THE

Bestiarius 'the Beast Fighter'
Weapons: spear and knife
Shield: small
Helmet: a visored helmet, the galea
Armour: basic leather arm and leg
    wraps
Opponents: wild animals including
    tigers, leopards and lions

Venator 'the Hunter'
Weapons: hunting spear, bow and arrows
Shield: none
Helmet: none
Armour: padding on arms and legs
    (optional)
Opponents: He does not fight, but
    hunts wild beasts and performs
    tricks with trained animals

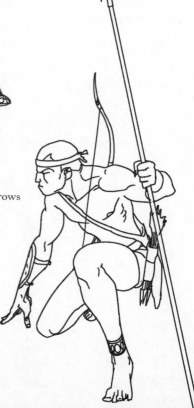

GLADIATORIAL ARENA

Laquearius 'the Snarer' (a type of Retiarius)
Weapons: dagger and lasso (laqueus)
Shield: none
Helmet: none
Armour: arm guard worn over left
  shoulder
Opponent: Secutor

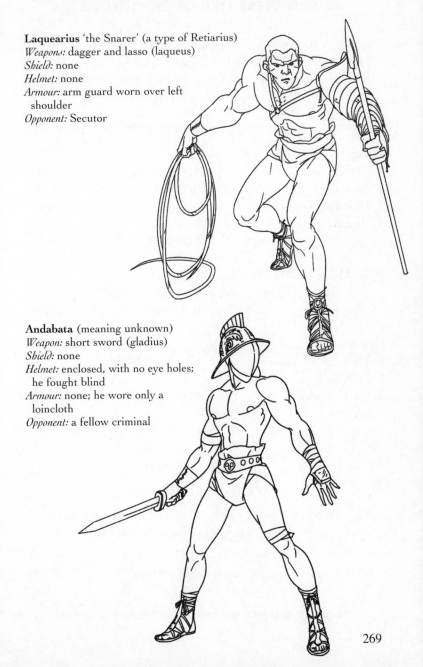

Andabata (meaning unknown)
Weapon: short sword (gladius)
Shield: none
Helmet: enclosed, with no eye holes;
  he fought blind
Armour: none; he wore only a
  loincloth
Opponent: a fellow criminal

A selected list of Scribo titles

The prices shown below are correct at the time of going to press. However, The Salariya Book Company reserves the right to show new retail prices on covers, which may differ from those previously advertised.

Gladiator School by Dan Scott

1 Blood Oath	978-1-908177-48-3	£6.99
2 Blood & Fire	978-1-908073-60-3	£6.99
3 Blood & Sand	978-1-909645-16-5	£6.99
4 Blood Vengeance *(Summer 2014)*		
	978-1-909645-62-2	£6.99

Aldo Moon by Alex Woolf

1 Aldo Moon and the Ghost at Gravewood Hall		
	978-1-908177-84-1	£6.99

Chronosphere by Alex Woolf

1 Time out of Time	978-1-907184-55-0	£6.99
2 Malfunction	978-1-907184-56-7	£6.99
3 Ex Tempora	978-1-908177-87-2	£6.99

Visit our website at:

www.salariya.com

All Scribo and Salariya Book Company titles can be ordered from your local bookshop, or by post from:

The Salariya Book Co. Ltd,
25 Marlborough Place
Brighton BN1 1UB

Postage and packing **free** in the United Kingdom

ABOUT THE AUTHOR

Dan Scott was born in Surrey, England. Growing up, he became interested in ancient Rome and, combining this with his hobby of reading historical fiction, he had plenty of inspiration for the adventure stories he first began to write as a child. Eventually, his characters and stories developed into the action-packed Gladiator School series.

When he's not writing, Dan enjoys rock climbing, visiting museums and collecting vintage guitars. He also spends too much time wishing he was a gladiator and fighting with his pet cat, Noxii.